WALK THE STARS

ROBERT WRIGHT

Copyright © 2016 Robert Wright

All rights reserved.

ISBN: 1533564817
ISBN-13: 978-1533564818

Cover design by Sherrie Wright

This is a work of fiction. Names, characters, businesses, places, events and incidents are either the products of the author's imagination or used in a fictitious manner. Any resemblance to actual persons, living or dead, or actual events is purely coincidental.

DEDICATION

To Sherrie & Scott who willingly compete with
the voices for my attention.

Witch Way series
Witch Way Home
Witch Way Back
Witch Way to Haven (Fall 2016)

Walk the Stars series
Walk the Stars

Ruby Red series
Ruby Red and the Wolf (Early 2017)

CONTENTS

Book 1: Ecstasy

Saying Goodbye	1
Preacher Speaks	12
Preparing to Run	22
Jolly's Story	33
Jim's Nightmare	45
An Alien Comes Calling	55
On the Run	69
Unexpected Help	81
Big Booms in the Night	95
Island Hopping	108
Meeting the Tekis	124
A Long March	141
Finding the Ship	152

Book 2: Emma

Emma	171
Questions and Answers	184
Throwing Rocks	196
Revenge	208
Billy	219
Folding Space	232
Bugs!	244
Rescue	258
Finding Earth	273

ACKNOWLEDGMENTS

Thanks to the friends and family who encouraged and supported this book. To my chief editor, cover artist, manager, and favorite fan – thanks for all the hard work you did and for putting up with the attitude I inflicted on you (for a third time) and hopefully it's getting better. Also thanks to my youngest who keeps me grounded.

BOOK 1
ECSTASY

Saying Goodbye

My tears matched the falling raindrops that dripped off the umbrella I stood under. I listened to the slow murmur of the preacher as he said comforting things about my parents, who lay side by side before the gaping holes ready to receive their coffins.

As I watched, the water unsurprisingly soaking all those around me as it had every day since I was born. I thought how the rain was a constant companion on this world we lived on. I mean here on Ecstasy it pretty much rains every day. My momma told me of other worlds where you see the Sun shining in clear blue skies. Sometimes I wonder if those were just some bedtime stories she made up.

As the preacher rambled on with his sermon, the feeling washed over me how all this felt so wrong. Not so much that as a teen I was now all on own, no parents to guide me through the rest of my life. It was more that the coffins that lay before me were just symbols, empty of my parents' bodies. They had never been found, for everyone knows that Teki raiders don't leave the dead on this planet.

No, that wasn't what was bothering me either; it was that I couldn't see my parents' spirits, ghosts or whatever you want to call what we become after we die. Now don't roll your eyes, I know that people say that you can't see ghosts, but I can. I mean as I looked around the graveyard here I could see all kinds of ghosts moving around the grounds, all but my parents' ghosts that is.

Momma said that I had this sight since I was just a little baby. She and daddy would tell me how I sat in my chair and babbled away at the empty air like there was someone standing there. It wasn't until I was older when I could tell them about the ghost that I could see that they finally understood what was going on with me. Not that I told them all that I could do, though. A girl must have some secrets, plus I saw them glance at me with that look when I talked to, what to them, was empty air. No sense my parents' thinking their daughter really was crazy if they knew all the things I was able to do.

Looking at all the people standing around some holes in the ground, heads bowed, listening to Preacher talk, the idea suddenly strikes me that since I don't see momma and daddies' ghosts, they aren't dead. So we are all wasting our time and needed to find where my parents really were.

I hear Preacher stutter and stop in the middle of his sermon and the murmur of the mourners as they watch me walk off into the rain, headed for the ground cars lined up at the side of the road. My cousin, who I love dearly, puts her hand on me as I pass, but I shrug it off and keep to my intended course.

One rough, deep voice breaks through the muttering of the small crowd bouncing off my back. "Cassie, where are you going?"

I ignore this voice as I always have since the person that belongs to this irritating noise had entered my life as my guardian two days ago.

"Cassie, I'm talking to you." The voice is now over my shoulder as I feel a large, beefy hand land on my arm pulling me to a sudden stop from my determined tracks away from the gravesites behind me.

I slowly turn and look up at the bloodshot little beady eyes that stare back down at me. "My momma and daddy aren't dead and I'm going to wait in the car."

The big man that is my uncle, my momma's brother, my cousin's father, looks back at the crowd at the gravesite and then back to me as he slowly bends his colossal bulk down to my level. "Listen, Cassie, I know this is hard, but your parents are gone. Now come back and we can let Preacher finish his sermon."

I shiver a little, not knowing if it is the cold rain that is now soaking me through the Sunday outfit I wear or the thought that this huge mountain of a man is now my guardian. "I am going to the car to wait, so let go of me now," I whisper, giving him the coldest stare I can muster for a seventeen-year-old.

My uncle glances over his shoulder at the crowd still standing at the gravesites and sees that causing a scene now would do him no good. Slowly a small sneer crosses his face as he lets go of my arm and stands up. "Yes well since you are feeling sick you go right ahead and wait in the car."

I turn without correcting him or saying anything else and head to the car to wait out the rest of Preacher's sermon. In the background, I can hear my uncle as he heads back and talks to several of the people about how I was so overcome with emotions that I fell ill.

Whatever, I think, as I climb into the car. Like I care what people think of my actions. As I sit there in the quiet of the car, I think how it doesn't matter really what my uncle says – most people on this planet think I'm strange anyway, so what should I care what they think of how I act today.

It is almost as cold in the car without the heater running as it is outside, but at least I am out of the rain. In fact, except for my cousin Rose and my parents, no one on this planet would give a damn about me. (I know not nice language for a kid my age.) Well, that's not right either. Preacher is nice to me even though at times he does give me those strange stares, almost like he knows my secrets or maybe he has secrets of his own.

I must have dozed off with my thoughts because I startle awake as I hear car doors open and close up and down the road. I keep my eyes closed as I feel the ground car shift as my uncle and Rose climb inside ready to drive us home.

As we arrive at our home, I peek from under closed eyelids at my house and see that there is already a crowd gathered on the porch waiting for our arrival. "Listen to me kid," my uncle whispers as he parks and shifts his weight to face me. "I know you are awake, so stop pretending."

I slowly look up at him, but don't answer as I look back out at the crowd invading my home.

My uncle sighs as if he is burdened by the world. "Fine be that way, but I'm warning you now if you cause any problems for me you will regret it. You do understand, right?"

I sit tight, not giving him the satisfaction of any reaction until I feel his hand grab my arm and squeeze it hard, naturally, out of sight of the people standing about. I can see Rose jerk in the front seat in fright, or maybe it's the memory of her own pain given by her father for, of course, I know that she has been on the receiving end of this treatment herself. "I said, do you understand, kid?" my uncle growled.

Giving a small gasp of pain, I give in for now but chalk this up on a running tally that this hated man is now running with me. "Yes, I get it. Now let go of me."

That sneer again as he goes to open the door of the ground car. "Fine, just so we understand each other and you play nice for the rest of the day. Now let's go in and greet the mourners of your dear old mom and dad."

Rose looks over at me as her daddy shuts the door and moves toward my home. "It's better, Cassie, for the both of us if you don't anger him," she whispers before she slides out of the car, shuts the door and slinks up the path behind the man I hate most in this world.

Yeah, well, your daddy is in for a surprise if he angers me anymore, I think, as I follow her lead and exit the old ground car.

As the dreary day runs into night, I slide through the ever-changing crowd that invades my house, listening to the people that smile at you with sympathy while inside they feel nothing for the strange little girl and her equally different parents.

Granted, when people needed my momma or daddy for their doctor skills they were Johnny on the spot to get their help, but for the most part, people treated them as outcasts or gave them the evil eye as they passed.

I sat in the corner thinking how Momma used to tell me it was because the world we lived in was reverting back, losing any advancements gained ever since she could remember. She said that her great-great grandmother had told that when she was a little girl that great ships would come from other worlds, to rescue the lost, but then Momma always was good at telling fairy tales.

I was jerked out of my thoughts as I focused on the people around me and started to listen to the conversations again. I slowly slid out of the small chair I was sitting on and glided over to the huge mountain of a woman that was the center of the biggest crowd in my living room. She was Mrs. Pug, even though there never seemed to have been a Mr. Pug, holding court and as always spewing trash from her mouth.

"I don't know how Jim will handle such a strange one like her, I mean doesn't he have enough to care for with his own daughter, Rose," she said as I heard murmurs of agreement from those around her.

I started away, not really caring what that old windbag said, but stopped as I heard her continue with her tirade on my cousin while stuffing her face with food from the large plate held in her chubby fingers. "I mean here the poor man has had to raise such a burden and now he is saddled with a second," she said crunching down on a protein stick.

I frowned at her and slowly backed away from the crowd and then moved back to my chair, all the time fuming at her words. People can talk about me all they want, but to hurt and talk about my quiet cousin like that required some payback.

As I sat there once more in the corner, I closed my eyes and slowly opened my mind, allowing myself to hear all the thoughts around me flow through my own. Then I focused on the one I was looking for, slowly sliding in seeing the dark aura of her thoughts, feeling the greasiness and the blackness of them rubbing off on my own mind.

I toughened up the walls of my mind, as her thoughts slowly slid off my defenses, looking for the one thing that she was most afraid of, for in my experience the blacker or darker the thoughts the more you fear the world around you.

There, that will do, I thought, as a small secretive smile slid onto my face. I watched as Mrs. Pug slowly picked up another protein stick, never looking down at what she was putting in her mouth since she was so busy spewing trash from it.

I pictured a stinker bug in my head, a nasty smelling bug that when squashed let out a horrendous smell that was hard to get rid of. I pictured that bug in her hand and watched as the protein stick that was now being bitten into turned into a stinker bug.

I opened my eyes and watched the commotion as people around Mrs. Pug covered their mouths and noses, some from the smell that now arose from the woman, and some from the half-eaten bug and the other mess that was now spewing from Mrs. Pug's mouth.

I don't know what was more funny, watching the wide, bug-eyed stare of Mrs. Pug as she looked down at the half-eaten bug that was wiggling on the floor in the mess she had made or the reaction of the people that were trying to get out of the door of the house to escape the sudden putrid smell that now invaded the room.

I looked up as a large shadow now filled my corner and saw my uncle looking down at me with anger. The laughter that seconds ago rang from my lips was swallowed back down as I looked at his dark face. "You did this, I know you did," he accused.

I gave as innocent a look that an innocent could give in this situation. "Who me? I've been sitting over here all this time. I don't know what you're talking about," I said. I guess I shouldn't have been laughing as hard as I was, damn.

"Don't give me that, girl. I know this is your work. I remember the times when your parents were alive and this kind of stuff used to happen to me," he said as he grabbed my arm and pulled me off my chair not even pretending anymore that he cared if anyone saw him hurt me.

I looked down at his hand on my arm and quietly with as much menace I could raise in my voice I said, "If I were you I would let go of my arm."

My uncle stood there, the anger warring with reason as he was clearly trying to think of some way to hurt me without repercussions. But he was slowly realizing that we were now drawing some attention to our corner of the house since most of the commotion was now dying down when a stern voice sounded from behind him.

"I think, Jim, that you should let her go," Preacher said as he laid a hand on my uncle's shoulder.

My uncle turned and looked at Preacher, his eyes still full of anger, but he slowly let go of my arm. I shrugged my shoulder and looked at the bruises that were now forming on my arm.

"It's her, Preacher, she did this," my uncle growled at him.

Preacher looked at me and then back toward my uncle and smiled. "So you are telling me that this young girl who was over in this corner somehow got a stinker bug into Mrs. Pug's dish, is that what you are telling me, Jim?"

My uncle glanced back and forth at me and Preacher and then over at Mrs. Pug who by this time was sitting on a couch across the room with some other old biddies around the poor stressed lady. I knew well enough to keep a smile off of my face, but believe me, it was hard.

My uncle took one last look at me and then shrugged Preacher's hand off of his shoulder. Walking away, he turned and pointed at me and in a loud voice said, "I know it was her, Preacher, she's no little innocent angel and someday everyone will see it, mark my words." And with that, he walked out of the house, slamming the front door.

Preacher looked after my uncle until he was gone and then turned toward me. "That wasn't very smart, Cassie. People around here are wary of you as it is."

I started to deny any wrongdoing but clamped my mouth

shut as Preacher gave me one of his soul searching looks. I stood there for a second and then shrugged my shoulders as I saw my cousin, Rose, starting to clean up the mess left on the floor by Mrs. Pug.

I moved to help her when Preacher reached down and blocked my way with his arm. "I think maybe, Cassie, it would be a good idea to go up to your room; I'll help Rose clean up."

Looking around the room and seeing the looks thrown my way by the few people that were still there, I thought that maybe Preacher had a point. "Alright if you say so, Preacher," I said as I headed for the stairs that lead up to my room.

"Oh, and Cassie," Preacher said in a quiet voice as he followed me to the bottom of the stairs, "I will talk to your uncle to watch his temper, but try to not cause trouble while I'm not here to help you. Think you can do that?"

I gave the preacher my most innocent smile and started up the steps. "Sure, Preacher, I'll try," I threw back at him with a small laugh.

Preacher Speaks

A couple of hours later I was still laying in bed. I had thrown myself on it when I came into the room and after I had turned on the small space heater to chase the chill of the day away. I listened as the last of the visitors left our home and I could just make out three voices still downstairs talking.

I quietly slid off my bed and peeked out my door when I heard the sound of feet shuffling up the wooden steps of the house. Seeing that it was Rose walking up the stairs I threw open the door and gave my cousin a big smile.

Rose stopped and looked up from her shuffling feet and then moved past me without any reaction. I watched as she headed into my room and threw herself on my bed. I was tempted to follow her but heard the mumble of two voices downstairs so I inched my way toward the top of the stairs to listen in on the conversation below.

I slowly looked around the corner of the wall and could see that I was looking down into our living room where

Preacher and my uncle were standing not two feet from each other. Preacher stood there with a stoic look on his face where my uncle wore his usual scowl.

I reached out with my mind and slowly probed the two of them, feeling for what they feared but was surprised in that all I got from Preacher was a blank spot – almost as if no one was there. What the heck? This had never happened to me before, I thought, so I leaned back around the corner and up against the wall as I closed my eyes and concentrated even harder on the two men below me.

I could feel my uncle's fear, a fear of long tentacles that were choking him to death. Well, okay that was weird as no creature on Ecstasy had those kinds of appendages. Then I shifted my focus to the other adult in the room, Preacher, but try as I might no matter how hard I concentrated all I came up with was that damn blank spot where he stood.

I opened my eyes and thought that maybe it was just something wrong with my mind then decided that I had better listen to what they were saying just in case their conversation involved little old innocent me. (Yeah, I know, you can stop snickering now.)

"Listen, Preacher, I don't like all this sneaking around. I want to renegotiate our deal," I heard my uncle say with a little fright creeping into his voice. Now I really had to pay attention to this conversation in that anything that scared my big bully of an uncle may not be good for me.

"Jim, Jim why do you think you have anything to

renegotiate with?" Preacher said in a sweet oily voice that seemed to float in the air.

"It's just that I seem to be the one hanging out on the edge in this little deal here."

Suddenly the fright of tentacles flared in my uncle's brain to such a high level that I saw it as clearly as if I stood right there in the room. I was just going to look down into the living room once more when I heard what sounded like a body hit the wall just below the stairs.

I moved up the steps quiet as I could so that I wouldn't be seen, but still hear what was happening down in the living room. Listening to a low gurgle and raspy breath and then the harsh whisper of Preacher, "The deal is that you find the part of the star map I need and I let you live. You do understand Jim, do you not?"

There was another small thump and then it sounded like something heavy slid down the wall. "Yeah, I get it, Preacher, please no more," my uncle's voice came out as a harsh whisper from below me.

Over the sound of something being lifted off the ground, I could hear Preacher's harsh whisper again. "That's good Jim, just so we all understand each other."

It was quiet now for a second and then I could hear someone move toward the door so I quickly moved further up the stairs and toward the upstairs hallway. The front door opened and I could see the bottom of Preacher's feet from where I stood. "Oh and Jim?"

"Yes, Preacher?"

"Leave the girls alone, both of the girls, you do understand don't you?"

"How I treat my kin is my business, Preacher, and not any part of the deal," my uncle said as his voice rose into his bully mode.

Preacher feet stepped toward him then stopped as I heard a small squeaking sound from my uncle. "If I see any more bruises on the girls, Jim, I will find someone else to handle our deal. Do you understand me now?" Preacher's voice once again sounding in that weird harsh whisper I heard before.

"Yes, Preacher, I understand. I won't touch the girls anymore," my uncle whispered so quietly that I barely heard his answer. "But what is it to you what I do to them girls? It's not like you care about our species."

"The reasons are mine that is all you have to know."

"Alright, Preacher, I said I would leave them alone."

"Fine, Jim, then you have two days to find the map," Preacher said as I watched him walk out the door.

I listened for a few minutes as my uncle smashed some stuff downstairs, but couldn't glean anymore from him so I moved as quiet as I could into my room. I looked over at my cousin as I closed the door and saw that she had changed into her P.J.s and was lying on her side on my bed. Now just what had my uncle meant by our species when he talked to Preacher, I thought, as I moved further into the room.

Ever since she was little, Rose's daddy would drop her off with my parents dragging my aunt off on some stupid venture. Rose would share my room and even my clothes and toys since she never had much of anything. Since she was a few months younger than me she was the sister I never had.

I quietly changed into my own night stuff and climbed into the bed thinking over and trying to make sense of what I had heard below in the living room while trying to not wake my cousin.

"I'm up," a small timid voice issued from the dark. "No need to be so quiet."

"Oh sorry, didn't want to wake you," I said to the dark that now filled my room.

It was quiet in the night until I heard a quiet sniffle sounding in the dark. I turned in the bed and wrapped my cousin in my arms and now the tears came flowing from her gaunt face and covered my nightshirt with their wetness as she turned toward me.

"It's alright, Rose," I said trying to comfort my cousin.

"No it's not, Cassie, you always get away with things and I'm the one that gets stuck cleaning up and catching the brunt of the grownup's anger."

I laid quietly listening to my cousin cry and thought over what she had said and figured that she was right. Rose was the one that usually got the sore end of the deal when I pulled some stunt on her dad or any other grown up for that matter. Heck even momma and daddy had their moments of frustration with me even as much as I knew that they loved me.

"I'm sorry, Rose. I'll try to do better, really I will."

Rose looked at me through the little light that filtered through my bedroom window as her tears dried up. "Promise me, Cassie, that you won't cause any more trouble with my dad. Lately, for some reason, he seems even worse than usual, almost like he is scared of something or someone."

I thought back to what I had heard down in the living room between Rose's daddy and the Preacher and thought to myself that I had a pretty good idea who my uncle was afraid of. "I will really, really try, Rose, I promise. Besides I heard the Preacher tell your daddy that he was not to touch us so we should be alright."

Rose shook her head and buried her head again into my shoulder so that I barely heard what she replied. "My dad won't listen to anyone, Cassie, not even to Preacher."

"Oh, I think he will listen to Preacher, Rose."

Rose looked at me with some small bit of anger shining through her eyes. "You don't know what my dad can be like, Cassie, you were lucky to have parents like you had."

"Come on, Rose, I know that your dad can be an as. . ."

Rose sat up as I was talking and shoved the sleeves of her P.J.s up both arms. The bruises that ran up and down her arms shut my mouth as I looked at the black and blue marks. "Oh, Rose, we need to tell someone what he did to you," I said in horror.

"No, Cassie, please don't. The last time someone said something it only got worse. You know how people around here are. No one cares what happens to others on this planet."

"Yeah, I know, Rose, I remember how hard it was to get someone out to look for my parents."

Rose looked down at the blankets on the bed and then back up at me. "My dad said it was because your parents were on the Teki Reservation, and no one is supposed to go there."

I sat there silently wondering how much I should tell my cousin about why my parents had gone off to the one place on this planet that was off limits to humans. The Teki were natives to Ecstasy and lived on one of the large islands on this planet that were set aside for their use.

My momma told me that after humans arrived on this planet there was a big fight between the Tekis and us and there was finally an uneasy peace created when we moved to the smaller of the two islands that made up the only really large land masses on Ecstasy.

"I'll tell you why they went there, Rose, but you need to keep it to yourself; in fact, you can't tell anyone – especially not your dad."

Rose looked at me and I could see a small smile light up on her face. "Don't worry about that, Cassie, I never tell my dad anything," she said as she looked down at her arms and the smile disappeared from her face. "Especially when he really wants to know something."

I sat up and hugged my cousin and was happy to see that she had enough gumption in her after all to stand up to her dad.

"I heard my daddy and momma say something about them finding a star map and that there is a Human spaceship on the Teki Reservation."

Rose's eyes got big as she sat there in stunned silence for a few minutes before voicing her thoughts. "But, Cassie, my dad said there are no such things as spaceships; that we are all on our own on Ecstasy, and that all the other planets got wiped out in some big war or something a long time ago."

"My momma told me that too, but then my parents found

where the original spaceship was, the one that brought our people to Ecstasy."

We both sat there for a couple of minutes thinking about a ship that could fly in space. Me thinking about how nice it would be to climb in a ship that would take me off this water-soaked rock; Rose lost in her own thoughts about such a ship.

"Yeah, but even if there is a ship now that your parents are dead there is no way anyone can find it ever."

I looked at my cousin and smiled a sly little smile. "Yeah, you would be right if my parents were dead, but I know they aren't dead so starting tomorrow I'm going to go and find them."

"Um, Cassie, I know you love your parents and you were close and all, but they are. . ."

I grabbed Rose's arms and shook her a little to stop her from finishing her thought, then looked down at her bare bruised arms and slowly let her go feeling bad about my reaction. "Sorry, Rose," I whispered.

Rose's eyes went blank as she looked at me and one small tear slid down her cheek. "I'm really sorry," I said as she laid down on the bed with her back to me.

Great, I thought, here I go and unintentionally hurt my only ally; the one person who I thought would help me find my parents and this ship of theirs. "I really am sorry, Rose," I said as I turned over on my side of the bed.

As I laid there every once in awhile I could hear a small sniffle come from my cousin's side of the bed and I wanted to turn and comfort her but wasn't sure how she would react, then soon it was quiet in the night and Rose slept. I lay there in the dark with my own thoughts intertwining through my head until I slowly followed my cousin down into that deep abyss of sleep.

Preparing to Run

I awoke, alone in my bed, listening to the patter of rain drumming its sad, dreary song on the roof of my home. Lying there, I could tell that the day would be like one of three types of days on this planet – one, cloudy with no rain; two, cloudy with drizzle; or three, cloudy with heavy rain.

I thought back to the stories that my momma told me about how her great-great-grandmother described the way the warmth of the sun felt on the face or how on some planets there were spots that never even saw rain or water for weeks, months, or sometimes even years.

I know it was probably just some fairy tale to tell us kids, but when you are never dry and all you can sniff in the air is the underlying smell of mold wherever you go a girl has to have hope in her life that there is something different than the world she knows.

Pretty soon I could hear the heavy footsteps of my uncle as he climbed the stairs to my room, fighting over the sounds of the rain that was now increasing in its ferocity. The door banged open hitting the wall and bouncing half way back toward my uncle as he stepped into the room. I couldn't help but jump from under the covers as my uncle moved toward the bed, a small growl leaving his lips.

"Get up you lazy brat, and get downstairs."

"I'm getting up; I'll be right down there."

My uncle raised his hand as though to hit me, but stopped at my next words. "Remember Preacher said you aren't to touch us."

My uncle stood there and looked at me for a second and then lunged across the bed and grabbed me by the front of my nightshirt and lifted me in the air so that I was looking him eye to eye, my feet hanging inches off the floor.

"Were you listening into our conversation, girl?" my uncle whispered, his sour smelling breath rolling over my face.

"No, no of course not, I heard some whisper about the Preacher saying that you couldn't hurt Rose or me."

My uncle stood there with me still hanging in the air his fist wrapped in the front of my nightshirt, his red eyes looking deep into mine. After what seemed like hours, but was only seconds my cousin's voice sounded from downstairs. "BREAKFAST IS READY," she yelled up the steps.

My uncle threw me down in the middle of my bed and stood there, a look of puzzlement or thought fighting across his face with the anger, and fear I could sense within him. Finally, the anger won out and he turned toward the door and stomped out of the room throwing over his shoulder, "Get dressed and get downstairs now, child, if you know what is good for you."

I laid there trying to get my heart to beat at its normal rhythm as I listened to him hit the stairs with those large boots making each wooden step tremble from his weight. As he hit the bottom step, I sprung out of bed and slammed the bedroom door and raced over to my dresser to get some clean clothes to throw on.

I wasn't sure how I was going to go about finding my parents, but I knew deep down that I needed to go to where they had been last seen, and that was on the Teki Reservation. I threw some outdoor clothes, and what little money I had in a waterproof pack and then opened my window and tossed it down into the hedge that surrounded most of the house. I figured it was safe enough as my uncle would never leave the dry warm house to go out in the rain that was now pouring down from the sky.

I grabbed a wicked little survival knife that my parents had given me on my last birthday and strung it on the back of my belt so that it would be covered by the large oversized sweatshirt I was wearing. I still had no plan on how to get across the water to the Teki Reservation, but at least I felt that I was ready for anything. Boy was I wrong on that count.

Just as I started down the stairs, my uncle turned the corner from the living room and looked up at me. "Lucky thing you were coming down, girl, for it saved me the trip up to drag you down here."

I smiled as I walked down the stairs and as I passed him said in a singsong voice, "Remember what Preacher told you."

All I got was a low growl from my uncle, but in some small part, I felt I had won a point. I walked into the dining room and saw breakfast laid out on the table, no doubt by my cousin, and sat down at the table and started to dish out what was in the bowls to my own plate.

Rose sat there eating quietly as her dad came in and took his own seat and started in where he had begun on his meal. The only sounds in the dining room where those of the spoons and forks scraping the dishes and the loud open-mouth chewing from my uncle, geez a whole other reason to hate him.

When we were done, I got up with my cousin to help clean up the breakfast mess hoping that my small gesture would make up some for the way I had treated her last night, but my uncle seemed to have other ideas.

"Sit down, girl, Rose will clean up."

"That's fine, I should help her since she made the breakfast," I said as I climbed out of my chair and started to pick up my dishes.

"I SAID SIT DOWN, GIRL!" my uncle bellowed, slamming his fist down on the table. A glass that was set on the edge of the table fell to the floor and shattered and then there was quiet as the two of us stared at my uncle.

I cocked my head and looked at him. "Really you're going with throwing temper tantrums now, uncle?"

I could see Rose as she moved behind my uncle shake her head at me, and then I remembered the promise I had made to her about not causing any trouble with her dad.

"You're right, uncle, I'm sorry," I whispered as Rose gave me a small smile and headed into the kitchen to get a broom and dustpan to clean up the glass scattered all over the dining room floor.

My uncle sat there for a couple of minutes looking at me with some suspicion written on his face then he let out a large sigh. "I need to ask you about your parents, Cassie."

"Uhm okay, what questions?"

"Do you know why your parents were over on the Teki Reservation?"

"No, sorry, I don't."

My uncle sat there looking at me like he didn't believe me at all. I sat quietly waiting for his next question.

"Okay then, did your parents ever mention a map?"

"What kind of map?" I asked.

"It really doesn't matter what kind of map, did they ever say anything about a map or maybe a ship?

By this time Rose had come back into the dining room and she stopped and turned sheet white and let out a small gasp at her dad's question. My uncle turned to Rose and looked at her with an irritated stare. "What's the matter with you now, girl?"

"Nothing, daddy," Rose answered as she quickly bent down to sweep up the broken glass.

My uncle turned back to me after watching his daughter for a few seconds and sat there waiting for an answer to his question.

I sat there looking like I was thinking about his question for a few seconds before I answered. "Uhm, no, nothing about any map or ship or anything like that."

My uncle stared at me and then shook his head and muttered under his breath about this being a waste of time as he got up from the table and headed into the living room and our com center.

"He knows, Cassie," Rose whispered from the floor.

I shushed her with my hands as I turned to watch my uncle sit down at the com center and pull up the hush hood so that we could not hear who he was calling or what he said. "Later," I whispered to Rose and then got up from the table to help her clean up the mess from our breakfast.

Later in the afternoon Rose and I were playing an old flying fighter game on my computer while her dad had disappeared somewhere into the back of the house. The computer I had was old as most of them were on this planet and it contained the only flying game that I knew of. The game was some old space war game, from when momma said we first came to this planet, where you flew a spaceship around these planets shooting down an alien armada.

It was a fun game in that you could play at any level from controlling your own armada to a single fighter. I was better at the commanding part of armada fighting where Rose was a much better fighter pilot with her quicker reflexes.

At a pause in the game, Rose leaned over and whispered, "Do you think my dad knows about the spaceship, Cassie?"

I stared at the computer screen waiting for the game to load the next section of the game as I thought about her question. Someone knew something about what my parents were looking for; I didn't think that Rose's dad was smart enough to make my parents disappear on his own.

"Yeah, Rose your dad knows what is up, and that's why I am out of here, later on, tonight."

"Where are you going, Cassie?"

I looked at Rose and tried to figure if I could still trust her. Ever since I helped her this morning clean up after breakfast she acted like she had forgiven me for grabbing her last night and we seemed to be back to being best friends again, but it was her dad we were talking about keeping secrets from.

"Alright I'll tell you, but you have to promise not to say anything to anyone and that means your dad also."

"I promise," Rose said as she crossed her fingers over her heart.

"Okay," I said smiling at my cousin's attempt to be serious. "I'm leaving tonight to find my parents and this ship of theirs."

"Why wait until tonight, Cassie?"

"Because I want to get into my parent's workshop and see if they left any clues to where they were going."

"Oh okay," my cousin said then she sat quietly for a few seconds and then looked at me with concern. "Are you coming back, Cassie?"

I sat there thinking about her question before answering. "No, I don't think so. I think that if my momma and daddy found this ship we would leave this backward planet. I think that is why they went to look for this ship."

"Then I want to go with you, Cassie."

Now it was my turn to look shocked at my cousin, the timid mouse that was scared of her shadow wanted to cross an ocean and follow me on some adventure. "You can't be serious, Rose?"

"I am. Look at me, Cassie, if you go my dad is going to be angry, and we both know who he will take that anger out on."

"But Rose we don't even know for sure there is a ship or not."

"I believe you, Cassie, when you say your parents are alive and I believe you that there is a ship too. The only thing we need to do is find out what your parents knew and where they went."

I smiled at my cousin and then winked at her. "That, my dear cousin, is why we need to get into my parent's workshop after your dad is asleep because I know someone in there that may be able to help us."

"Who will help us and I don't think we can get in there anyways."

"The who you will just have to wait and see, Rose, but what makes you think we can't get into the workshop?"

"Well when I came down to get breakfast, I saw my dad trying to get into the door but he couldn't get past the lock."

That image brought another small sly smile to my face.

"That won't be a problem, Rose; there is a door into the workshop for me that only I and my parents know about, sort of a hidey hole for me in case it was ever needed."

We jumped a little as we heard a creak of the floor outside my room as though someone had stepped on one of the loose boards outside my door. I put my finger to my mouth and walked toward my door and flung it open and looked up into the eyes of Preacher.

"Hello, girls, I stopped by to talk to Jim and to see how you two are doing," Preacher said a wide smile on his face, a smile that seemed to stop well short of his eyes.

"Hello, Preacher," we both answered together.

We all stood there in an awkward silence, the two of us looking at Preacher as we both wondered how much he had heard and if it really mattered to our plans.

"Well you girls seem fine so I will go back down and talk to Rose's dad and then head out on my rounds," Preacher said with a smile and then turned and headed down the stairs.

I shut the door of my room and went and sat down to play the game that had finally loaded once more when Rose let out a tight relieved breath. "I don't know what it is about him, but sometimes the way he looks at people, it's like how we look at a dog or a cow."

I thought over what my cousin had said but really couldn't agree or disagree with her since when my parents were around we never really had a lot of interaction with Preacher.

"Well after tonight we won't have to worry about Preacher or your dad, so don't worry too much about it, Rose."

"Okay," Rose said and as we played the loaded game again we forgot all about Preacher and Rose's dad.

Jolly's Story

The rest of the day was pretty uneventful except that we had to find Rose a waterproof pack and some clothes and drop it with my pack in the hedge. Rose, while making dinner later that night, also managed to pack some food for us to last a couple of days so that we could hide out without worrying about going hungry.

My uncle even seemed to be in a good mood at dinner and kept his voice down to a low growl when he was talking to us. After cleaning up after dinner and spending some time on the com center watching what little news came our way, both Rose and I headed to bed.

As we started up the steps, my uncle growled at us. "Tomorrow, Cassie, we need to get into your parent's workshop."

"Oh, why? Can't you open it, Uncle Jim?" I asked, the sweetness of my voice dripping into the air.

"No, but I think we will figure a way to open it," my uncle

said with a dark smile.

"Uhm, that is my parent's workshop and I know they didn't like people going in and messing with their stuff."

"Yeah, well, your parents are dead so get used to it, and we need to see what is in there."

"Oh, who are we, uncle?"

My uncle looked at me and the dark smile of his got bigger than before. "Don't you worry about that, girl; you get up to bed now."

I nodded not liking the way that my uncle was so confident about my parent's fate. When I got up to my room, I found that my cousin was already in bed under the covers.

"What did he want, Cassie?" she whispered.

"Just wanted to twist my tail a little I guess, Rose," I said as I set the timer on my watch for an eleven o'clock wake up. "Let's try to get some sleep, okay? We are going to have a long night ahead of us."

Rose nodded and turned on her side and was soon asleep. I lay there in the night listening to my uncle move around downstairs until it was quiet in the house and I felt myself drifting off into a deep slumber.

The small beeping sound of my watch pulled me from the deep well of sleep I had fallen down into, that and the insistent shaking of Rose's hands on my shoulders. "I'm up, I'm up," I mumbled as I opened my eyes to look at my cousin.

I looked up at her smiling face and groaned, oh how I hate morning people or middle of the night people as the case was with her. Then she bounced off the bed and twirled around in a circle and I laid there watching her.

"Why are you so peppy in the middle of the night?" I whispered.

Rose came over to the bed and threw herself on her back and smiled at the ceiling. "I'm happy because this is my last night here, Cassie."

I hated to kill my cousin's mood but brought her back down to the ground with my next words. "Yeah, well, let's not get ahead of ourselves there, Rose. First, we need to find out if we can see where my parents have gone to."

"Yeah, you're right, Cassie, sorry," Rose said as the smile of happiness left her face and she sat up on the edge of the bed. "Now what do we do?"

"Now we go down to my parent's workshop and talk to someone that may be able to help us."

"You said that before, Cassie, but we three are the only ones here. Who is going to help us?"

I got out of bed and started toward the closet in my room. "Don't worry about who is going to help, let's get this show on the road," I said as I opened the door of the closet and turned a small coat hook on the inside of the wall. There was a click and a small square of floor in the closet popped up a hair. I reached down and opened the door that looked down a small dark tunnel just big enough for the two of us to crawl down single file.

"Uhm a little dark isn't it, Cassie?"

"Yeah, sorry forgot," I said as I bent down on my knees and reached in and flipped a switch that sat under the edge of the tunnel. A soft glow lit up the night and showed a ladder attached to one wall of the tunnel.

"What the hel. . ."

"Rose, your language," I said laughing as my cousin stood there staring down the tunnel and blushing at the slip. "I think I am becoming a bad influence on you, cousin dear," I added quietly, laughing at the look she threw me.

I stopped laughing when I heard a creak outside my door. We both stood frozen listening to the house waiting for any more sounds, but all was quiet in the night. After a couple of minutes, I motioned Rose to follow me down the ladder. It was a tight fit, made that way purposely so that no adult could use the ladder and follow me down that way.

Once we were down on the floor, I hit a small switch next to the ladder and watched as the floor of my closet came down and clicked in place and the lights went out. Rose gave a small squeal but was quiet as a red light popped on seconds later.

"Sorry forgot about that part," I said with a smile as my cousin gave me a dirty look again.

"Fine now what?" Rose said as she looked around the tiny room we were in.

"Now this," I said as I walked up to a wall that faced into my parent's workshop. Reaching out, I slid open a small door and looked out into the workshop's interior.

"Uhm, Cassie, this is a little paranoid don't you think?"

I looked out the little window and then seeing that it was clear I closed it and turned to Rose. "My parents built this whole thing," I said throwing my arms out to encompass the little room and ladder, "as a precautionary measure because they didn't like how people were starting to act toward them. Besides being this close to the ocean there have been Teki raids through the years, so it is always better to be safe and have a hidey hole than not have one and be sorry."

"Yeah, I guess, Cassie," my cousin whispered with some doubt still in her voice.

"Don't worry, Rose, if everything goes good tonight it won't matter anyways, right?" I said as I hit a small button next to the wall.

The wall slid sideways and I walked into my parent's workshop hitting another light switch bringing a subdued light up into the room. Rose stared around at my parent's workshop, a shelf of books running along one wall from floor to ceiling; another wall that held different maps of Ecstasy, some that looked like they were taken from really far up, and the tables that held all kinds of junk and stuff that my parents had collected through their studies.

"Wow, are those real books?" Rose said in awe of my parent's library.

"Yeah, real books alright, my momma said that they were from the ship that brought us all here and it was my great-great grandmother's momma that saved them."

"Wow!" Rose whispered once more as she wandered over to look at the books more closely.

"Be careful with them, they can come apart easily," I said as I watched her start to reach out for the books and then pull her hands away from them as though they were on fire.

I smiled and then turned toward the room and called out in a low whisper, "Jolly? Where are you?" I waited, nothing but silence greeted me. "Jolly, I need to really, really need to talk to you," I whispered urgently.

Nothing but more silence for a few seconds and I was going to try again when a white mist started to form in front of me.

"WHAT IS IT, GIRL!?!" a loud voice sounded almost in

my ear.

"Sssh! Jolly, I need to ask you some questions, keep your voice down."

The gray figure of a man looked down at me and smiled. "Why? No one but you can hear me, girl."

"Oh yeah," I said. With everything on my mind, I forgot that little fact. "Sorry, but I'm in a bind and need your help."

"Uhm, Cassie, who are you talking to?" Rose asked as she backed up into the bookcase, her eyes going large with fright.

I looked at Rose with a smile of reassurance. "Remember when I said I could see and talk to ghosts a couple of years ago."

"Yeah?" Rose answered with some doubt in her voice.

"Well, Jolly is one of those ghosts, Rose."

"Yes and he is a ghost that does not like to be ignored by silly little girls. So if you are done, I have better things to do," Jolly growled.

"Uhm, Jolly, you are dead. What else do you have to do except hang around your burial spot?" I asked.

"You know, little girl, I rue the day that your parents built this house on sacred ground," Jolly said puffing out his chest and stalking around the room.

I gave a small laugh then covered it up with a cough into my hands. "Uhm sorry, Jolly, but like I told you before, you died while on the move to the original city the first people set up and there was no record of where you were buried."

"Yes, yes I know you said that before, but how they could forget such a person as me I will never know."

"Uhm, Jolly, the records say you were a garbage mate third class on a ship. You died because you ate some Ding berries which everyone told you not to eat." I heard Rose snicker behind me, as I tried to keep a straight face. No sense in making the ghost mad before we got our answers.

"Well yes, never mind all that. You said you have some questions you want me to answer, girl?" Jolly asked, a scowl crossing his pale face at having his importance questioned.

I smiled at Jolly and the indignation on his face, for the way to get him to focus on what I wanted to find out was to remind him of his position in life and how he had died. I really did feel sorry for him in that his burial place had been lost in the records and my parents just happened to build our home over it, but right now I needed some answers and only Jolly could give them to me.

"Okay, when my parents were in their workshop did you happen to hear them mention anything about a spaceship or a map, Jolly?"

"Well I never, little girl, to think that I would stoop so low as to listen in. . ."

I cut Jolly off with a look and waited. Man, this ghost could be so self-centered and annoying at times. Jolly looked at me and then down at the ground and then back up at me with a smile. "I guess you know me well, don't you, girl?"

"Yeah, Jolly, I know that you said you can't go anywhere else and that when I was in here with my parents you always hung on every word that was said by us."

"Yes well, it does get boring in here you know. You couldn't have built a com center here, noooo you had to build a workshop with books I can't even read."

"I'm really sorry Jolly, but I need to find some answers."

"Fine, little girl, I will tell you what I know. Your parents were in here one night by themselves, and they were talking about finding the original spaceship that flew us to this stupid planet where we crash landed."

"Oh, what good would that do anyone?"

"You see, little girl, even though the main ship was damaged, we carried two experimental scout ships in the cargo bay."

"Well, how come you guys didn't leave this planet on those ships then?"

Jolly shook his head in sadness, looking off into the past and then refocused on me. "We didn't leave for three reasons, little girl. First, there was the Tekis that attacked us as soon as we landed. Second all the command personnel of the ship were killed in the crash so that no one could fly the ships, except maybe the Captain's wife, but she would never leave all these people on their own."

"And the third reason?" I asked Jolly.

"The third reason is that each ship was only big enough for a crew of five people. We had over two thousand people alive after the crash."

"Uhm what kind of ship was this, Jolly?"

"Why an escape ship from the aliens, of course," Jolly said his pale face now set in grim lines.

"Aliens?" I said

"Aliens?" Rose echoed from by the bookcase.

"Well yes aliens, you do know about the aliens that were destroying all the outer rim planets and searching for our home world, Earth, right?"

"Uhm no," I answered.

"What do they teach you young children on this planet?"

"Well not much really, Jolly," I answered

"Is it, I mean, he or whatever telling you more about these aliens, Cassie?" Rose asked as she walked up beside me staring off into the general direction that Jolly stood.

"What a rude girl," Jolly said looking at Rose, that indignant look once again crossing his face.

I sighed and looked at Rose and whispered, "Sssh, we're getting there."

Then I turned back to my conversation with the ghost. "Showed up and started to destroy all the cities that were built on the outer rim worlds. We, of course, lived on Prosper, a planet that had just started showing a profit and managing on our own when the aliens hit us."

"And the ship you were on?" I asked as Jolly stopped talking and stared off into the air again.

"Yes, the ship . . . well just before we got hit by the aliens, a ship from Earth landed with a battalion of Marines on it, nasty big, loud men if there ever were some."

"And then what?" I asked as Jolly once again drifted off into his own thoughts once more.

"Oh yeah, sorry, well when they offloaded the Marines, they loaded all the people they could onto the ship, in fact, overloaded it if you asked me, and were headed for home when we got hit by the aliens. We made it out of the atmosphere and tried to make a run for it. The Captain finally got to a spot where we could use the drive engines, but I guess our navigation was gone and we ended up here on this rock."

"And the other people and the Marines on Prosper, Jolly? What happened to them?"

"Well, I guess that as nasty as the Marines were the aliens were worse. From what I gathered no one lasted long on the planet after the aliens reached the ground."

"Oh, I'm sorry, Jolly," I said as I saw the miserable look on the ghost's face.

"Yeah, well, that is well in the past, anyway as you wanted to know your parents found where the original ship was and were going there to see if they could get one of the scout ships to fly."

"Uhm, Jolly? Two questions – do you know where the ship is and why they wanted to find it?" I asked.

"Well, yes, the information you want is in the top drawer there," he said pointing to a small file cabinet in the corner. "And the why they wanted to find the ship is because the aliens have found you here on this planet."

Jim's Nightmare

I stood there thinking over what Jolly had said and some remembered thoughts niggling at the back of my head, but they were lost as I looked over at the cabinet and the combination lock on it.

"Uhm, Jolly, about that cabinet . . . uhm you wouldn't happen to know. . ."

"Ten left, two right, three left," Jolly said cutting off my question with a big smile on his face.

I looked at him as Rose went over to try the lock with the numbers I gave her. "Well so kill me for looking over your parent's shoulder. It's not like I'm going to tell anyone."

I looked at Jolly as I heard the lock click open and I raised an eyebrow and gave him a wicked smile.

"Oh yeah, I guess I told someone, you," he said with a small embarrassed look on his face.

Giving the ghost a friendly smile, I said, "Thanks anyway,

Jolly."

"Yeah, no problem, like I said what can they do? Kill me a second time?"

I went over to the cabinet and looked down at the contents inside it. There, under some small blasters, was a map of the island that was the Teki Reservation. I picked it up and looked at the map and saw that there was a large X marked next to a mountain in the middle of the island.

"Hey, Jolly, is this where you guys landed?" I asked, laying the map on one of the few empty tables in the workshop.

"Yeah, but it was more of a plowing in nose first into the side of a big mountain than what I would call an actual landing, little girl."

"You do know I have a name besides little girl, right Jolly?"

The ghost stood there looking down at me and smiled. I sighed and figured I needed to pick my battles and this was one I wasn't going to win. Rolling up the map, I walked back over to the cabinet and hefted out the two small blasters that were in the drawer.

"Uhm, Cassie, what are you going to do with those?"

"Well, you heard Jolly say there were aliens right?"

"Yeah?"

"Well okay then, we may need to have some protection against them, and if not for the aliens then we will need them for the Teki once we get over to their land."

"Cassie, I've never fired one of those before," Rose said looking with some fright at the blaster.

"No problem, my parents showed me how to shoot and reload them," I said as I walked over and strapped the belt holding the blaster, its holster and extra energy packs around my cousin's waist.

"There now, you look like a real adventurer," I said as I strapped my own weapon on.

"I don't really think you should go over to the Teki place, girls," Jolly said as he looked at us with some concern in his eyes.

"Yeah, well my parents are there and this ship is there so we are going."

Well, I guess it was nice knowing you, but I will miss talking to someone, just try not to get dead though it's not all that fun, little girl."

"Yeah, I'll try, Jolly," I said as Rose and I headed back toward the ladder that led up to my room, but a thought crossed my mind and I turned back to ask Jolly a question that was bothering me about his story.

"Uhm Jolly, why did the Captain of the ship come to Prosper to save the people?" I asked.

"Oh well, you see the Captain was going to retire soon to

Prosper and his pregnant wife was on there waiting for him. When the Captain heard that Earth was leaving the outer rim worlds to fend for themselves he took his ship and tried to help as many people as he could."

"Oh, and those Marines, that was what you called them, how about them? You said they stayed behind?"

Jolly looked down at the ground and whispered, "The Marines, big and nasty all of them, and each and every one of them knew it was a one-way trip. The bravest men I knew, for they took a lot of aliens down with them.

"Thanks, Jolly," I whispered back and then followed Rose back into the small room shutting the door behind me.

We were both quiet with our own thoughts as we climbed the ladder and walked into my room. I guess that is why we missed seeing my uncle standing in the open doorway of my bedroom. "So you girls find that map I was looking for?" my uncle growled from the dark doorway, making both of us jump five feet into the air.

I looked at the shadow that was my uncle and stepped back toward the closet door, dropping the map I held in my hands onto a small shelf that ran along the inside of it. While Rose walked up to her dad and flipped on the light switch by the door.

I had to give my cousin some credit, after her initial scare, she seemed to have put any fear behind her and was standing up to her dad. "I'm sorry dad, what map?"

My uncle looked at Rose and then growled at me. "Come here girl and give me the map. I know you have it."

I stepped away from the closet and walked into the middle of the room. "I don't know what I think you know, uncle, but I don't have a map."

"Yeah, she doesn't have a map," my cousin echoed.

Without saying a word my uncle turned and slammed my cousin into the wall, knocking over my bedside lamp behind my nightstand. The room went into a partial darkness as my uncle moved with greater speed than I thought he had and once more grabbed me by the front of my clothes and lifted me in the air until we were face to face.

"I want the map, girl, and I want it now," he said, his breath full of the smell of liquor washing over me.

I reached up and tried to pry his arms off of me, but that was like trying to move two solid bands of steel. Finally, I gave up struggling and hung in the air and then I did something that wasn't very smart but was satisfying to me – I spit in his face.

Well, at least it was satisfying until my uncle turned and hurled me into the wall next to my closet. I saw stars as I slowly slid down the wall and blackness descended over me before it quickly dissolved.

I watched from the ground as my uncle slowly wiped the spit off of his face and then gave me a nasty smile. "I gotta say, girl, you got spirit if nothing else. You are stupid, but you do have spirit, not like my wimpy kid here," he said as he glanced at Rose who had pulled herself up off the floor and was leaning on the bed.

"I HATE YOU, YOU'RE NOT MY REAL FATHER ANYWAYS!" my cousin yelled at her dad.

"Watch your mouth, Rose," my uncle growled.

"I don't have to listen to you, my mom told me before she disappeared that you weren't my real father. So you can go to hel. . ."

Once again with a surprising quickness my uncle had Rose by the neck cutting off her tirade and was now looking her in the eye. "You're right, little girl, I ain't your daddy and that's why your poor little mommy disappeared."

My uncle squeezed down on my cousin's throat and I heard her gasp, trying to breathe as he turned to face me. "Now, girl, tell me where the map is or your cousin gets the same thing her mommy got, understand me?"

"LET HER GO!" I yelled watching the feet of my cousin beat in the air as I slowly inched my hand toward the blaster on my hip.

My uncle had a big nasty smile plastered on his face as he

looked at me. "If you touch that gun, girl, I'll snap her neck. I did it to her mom and I'll do it to her."

I looked at my uncle and then I flashed again to what frightened him the most as I watched two large tentacles slide out from under the bed. One wrapped around his chest while the other slid around his neck and squeezed, cutting off the sudden yell of surprise he started to issue.

My uncle dropped my cousin on the floor and I rushed over to look to see if she was still alive. Watching her chest slowly rise and fall, I saw the blue color leave her face as she took in air.

I stood up and looked up at my uncle, watching his eyes almost pop out of his head as he tried to fight the two thick bands of strength that now held him in place.

"You know, uncle, I used to be afraid of this most terrible monster under my bed. It had these ten long tentacles that I thought would come out from under the bed and wrap me up." As I spoke, eight more slithering bands came out and wrapped around various parts of my uncle's body.

My uncle's eyes were now bulging out of their sockets with fear as the tentacles slammed his body to the ground and slowly, ever so slowly, started to pull him under the bed. "But what was the worst about this fear were the teeth that I knew was under the bed, uncle, the teeth that I just knew would slowly eat me, bit by slow bit," I said and I looked down as a large crunching sounded from under the bed.

My uncle tried to scream again, but the tentacle around his throat squeezed harder, cutting off the sound of his distress. I bent down to look at my uncle, eye to eye. "But I think you have taught me, uncle, that the worst monsters don't live under my bed at all," I said as his face disappeared into the darkness under my bed.

I stood up as a tentacle came out from under the bed and then set out to reach for me and I could swear I heard a small growl. "I'm not afraid of you anymore," I said as it hung in the air for a second and then slowly slid back under the bed.

I looked at the bed and then the floor, seeing a small trickle of red dribble out from the darkness. I smiled, turned and kneeled by my cousin to check to see how she was doing. "Rose wake up, are you still with me?" I asked raising her up to a sitting position as her eyes started to flutter open.

"Cassie, what happened?" she asked as she looked around the room. "Where is my dad?"

"Don't worry about your dad anymore. Can you stand up, Rose?"

"Yeah, sure. I just feel a little wobbly."

"Okay, then let's get you on your feet," I said helping my cousin stand up.

My cousin just stood there leaning against me for a few minutes as she got her breath back and the dizziness went away. "Uhm, Cassie, before I went black, I thought I saw something grab my dad from behind," Rose said looking me in the eyes.

I sighed and tried to figure out if I told her the truth would my cousin hate me or still love me. "Remember that one time when I had that terrible nightmare when you were sleeping over?"

"Yeah, I remember, Cassie," Rose said looking down at the edge of the bed and giving a little body shiver. "Oh!" she whispered as she spotted the small trickle of blood that seeped from under the bed.

We stood there in the quiet night, the idea of what I had done slamming into my cousin. "Uhm thanks, Cassie," she whispered once again.

"I'm not proud of it, Rose, but it was the only way to. . ."

Rose turned in my arms and hugged me, cutting off my breath and stopping what I was trying to explain to my cousin. "After what he did to my mother and me don't ever be sorry, Cassie," Rose whispered into my shirt.

"Come on, Rose, we need to get going if we are going to find my parents and this ship," I said as I moved away from my cousin and picked up the lamp from the floor and put it back on my nightstand.

"Now what do we do Cassie?"

"Well since we don't have your dad to worry about anymore," I said with a chuckle as we both looked at the bed. "I say we get our packs from outside, get some food together and then use the ground car to hit the port where we find a boat to go over to the Teki Reservation."

"Sounds like a plan. You get the packs and I'll get some more food together."

With that plan in mind, I headed over to the closet to get our map and then headed outside as Rose hit the kitchen. I figured if we were lucky we could be out of here in ten minutes. Surprising how unlucky I was tonight.

An Alien Comes Calling

Rose and I split some of my parent's field rations that we found in the kitchen between our packs. By the time we were done, we were both staggering under the load of full packs. I was definitely glad that we had decided to use the ground car to travel to the port.

While we had been raiding the kitchen, Rose didn't have a lot to say to me except respond to my questions with short yes and no answers. I thought maybe she was having second thoughts about accompanying me with what had happened up in the bedroom to her dad.

As we finished packing, Rose looked over at me with some concern lighting up her face. "Uhm, Cassie, I have a question for you, but I don't want you to take this wrong, okay?"

"Sure, Rose, what's the question?"

"Well this power of yours, I mean what you did with my dad?"

I cringed a little inside, thinking of it not so much as a power more like a curse. "Yeah, you mean being able to manifest people's fears into the real world?"

"Yeah, that. Well have you ever looked at my mind or wherever it is you see a person's fears come from?" Rose said as she stared down at her feet, her voice going down to a whisper at the end of her question.

I walked over to my cousin and cupped her face in my hands and made her look me in the eyes. "Rose, you and my parents are the only people that I would never, ever use this ability on, understand me?"

The concern left my cousin's eyes as she looked deep within mine and a bright smile that I hadn't seen in a long while lit up her face. "Yeah, okay, I believe you Cassie; I wanted to know for sure."

"Hey no problem, if it was me I would want to know what the crazy girl was up to, too," I said giving my cousin the same smile back that covered her face.

"You're not crazy, Cassie," Rose said, the smile now being replaced by a grim determined look.

"Well, I think people would say that a girl that talks to ghosts and can make people's fears come alive to eat them is not quite sane, wouldn't you?"

"Yeah, well, I still say you aren't crazy, Cassie, but one more question, please?"

"Sure Rose, shoot."

"Well, where did the fear that ate my dad come from? I didn't think he was afraid of anything."

"Part of the fear was your dad's because he was afraid of something with tentacles, but the main thing under the bed was my fear," I whispered.

"Oh yeah, you mentioned that the one night I slept over and you woke us all up in the middle of the night screaming your head off. I remember that night."

"Yeah, believe me so do I, Rose."

"I also remember that it took a lot for your parents to settle you down and that you refused to tell them what woke you up screaming like that. Was that what woke you up that night, Cassie?"

"Yeah, it was Rose. It was a nightmare that I was in a place that I couldn't escape, and that no matter where I went there were these huge monsters with long tentacles always reaching and grasping for me, trying to pull me into this large mouth full of teeth."

We both stood there in silence with that thought moving through our minds until my cousin broke the silent night with a whisper of her voice. "That's a scary dream to have, Cassie."

"Yeah, that's a major understatement Rose, but the feeling I have is I don't think it was a dream as much as a shared memory from someone that lived through something like that."

"But then how did you dream it, Cassie?"

"I don't know, Rose, all I know is that it was too real to be a dream. I think someone, one of my family that escaped the aliens actually went through what I dreamed about and it got passed down to this crazy mind of mine."

"Okay, I guess that makes some sense for you, right?"

"Right, Rose. Now enough talk and let's get out of here, that is if you are still coming with me, cousin?"

"Oh, I wouldn't miss this for the world, Cassie. Besides from what I heard from your talk with the ghost downstairs, the aliens are here or coming and I don't want to meet whatever lived under your bed in real life."

"Yeah, me neither, Rose, me neither. So let's go."

We headed out and got as far as the living room when Rose suddenly stopped and gasped. "Oh hey wait, my dad's stash, I almost forgot it."

I stopped by the living room couch and looked at my cousin in disbelief for it was getting late and we really needed to be on the road before anyone stopped by and checked on us. As big of a pain as my uncle had been, we would have been hard pressed to explain what had happened to him and all our plans would have gone up in smoke.

"Come on, Rose, we really don't have time for this."

"No, Cassie, we do, for my dad had a stash of cash in his room that he didn't know I knew about."

I stopped for a second and thought about it, then asked with some interest, "Oh? How much cash, Rose?"

A little sly smile crossed my cousin's face. "Last time I counted, he had about ten thousand credits."

"Where would your dad get that much money? He never worked a real job in his life and he doesn't seem to be the 'saving for retirement' type?"

"I don't know, Cassie, but I do know that he had a lot of money this last year and he built up this stash of money that he kept hidden from me, or at least he thought that he had kept it hidden," Rose said with a sly little smile crossing her face again.

Damn, who would have thought that my cousin was such a sneaky little bugger? "Okay well go and get it, we could sure use that kind of cash once we get to the port, but don't take too long; we should have already left this place."

"Okay, Cassie, be right back." And with that, my cousin ran into the back room of the house that my uncle had been using as a bedroom.

As soon as my cousin left the room, there was a knock on the front door. Oh hell, now we were in for it, I thought, as I dropped my pack behind the couch and walked over the door to see who would be here at this time of night.

I looked out of the little side window by the door and was surprised to see Jade, an apprentice of Preacher, and the basic nosey body of the town. It wasn't hard to know why Preacher knew everything that went down around this town when Jade always seemed to be where something was happening, no matter if it was bad or good.

I opened the door and looked out at him. "Yes, can I help you, Jade?"

"Yeah, it's Cassie, right? Preacher sent me to check up on you and your cousin."

"Uhm yeah, well, you can tell Preacher that me and Rose are fine."

"Well, Preacher also wanted me to talk to Jim too. Is he here?"

"Sorry he's not here right now, and my cousin and I were going to bed so I'm sure you can come back tomorrow," I said as I started to close the front door to the house, but that action was stopped by Jade's foot being in the way and then him slowly pushing the door open once again.

"Oh, now I don't think it would be responsible for me to leave two girls out here all on their own with no adult to protect them," Jade said as he moved past me and into the room.

"HEY!" I yelled. "You can't come and burst into my home like that."

"Oh don't worry; as soon as Jim comes home I'll leave. I'm sure Preacher would never want me to leave you two here by yourselves."

For some reason, I didn't like how this conversation was going on several levels. One was that my uncle was not going to come home or anywhere else for that matter and Rose and I really needed to get out of here and head to the port. The second reason was that Jade was giving me the creeps for some reason. I don't know if it was the way he was acting or that he seemed off for some reason, but deep down I knew I wanted him out of my house now.

"Listen, Jade, you are not an adult that belongs in this house and if you don't leave out that door now I'm getting on the com unit and calling the law," I said pointing at the still open door.

Jade stood there looking at me with a strange smile on his face. "Go ahead, Cassie, call the law."

I looked at Jade and then slammed the door and walked over toward the couch as Jade looked down at my hips with a question in his eye. "Why you wearing a blaster in the house anyways, girl, and just where is Jim?"

I stood there looking at Jade, figuring that maybe I could

come up with something to frighten him out of the house, but as I tried to search his mind all I came up with was a blank spot just like Preacher. "Why is it I can't read you?" I mumbled in a puzzled tone.

Jade took a few steps across the room before I could move and his fist hit me, knocking me sideways onto the couch. "I said where is Jim, girl?"

My head was ringing from the blow and it took a couple of seconds for my eyes to focus on the man standing above me. "I don't know where he went, and I wouldn't tell you anyways now."

"Oh, you will tell me, girl, one way or another you will tell me." As Jade said these words, the air around him seemed to shimmer and change and then I was looking at my worst nightmare come to life.

Where Jade had stood now a bug-eyed monster stood. I looked at those dead, unblinking eyes and knew that they held no concept of human mercy within their depths. Those eyes were mounted on a triangular, squid-like head with no nose, but a large mouth that showed rows upon rows of teeth that seemed to lead deep down into that dark gullet.

Oh, I was so in trouble now, I thought, as I took in the alien that stood there. "Now where is your uncle and where is the star map, girl?" the monster that was once Jade asked. The voice wasn't coming from his mouth, but from a tiny disk mounted on his throat.

"What the hell are you? Where is Jade?"

A small chuckle came out of the disk followed by Jade's voice. "Why when we take over a body we need to kill off the original. Can't take the chance of two of us running around now, can we?"

As my eyes focused and mind cleared, I noticed that the alien now had two tentacles where his arms were and I had a pretty good idea where my uncle's fear of these appendages had come from. Okay, no big loss, I thought, then felt bad, even if Jade had been a big pain around town. "Fine, but what are you and what map are you talking about?"

The thing that stood there before me just stared, studying me as we would a bug on the rug for a few seconds before answering. "We are a race that is taking back what is ours. You monkeys took our planets from us and we have to destroy such an infestation before you spread out anymore."

"What are you talking about? This isn't your planet; I know that there are no such creatures like you that live on Ecstasy."

"You are right, little one, this isn't our planet. In fact, it is well off into the far star system and it took us a long time to find where you monkeys ran to," the voice from the disk said.

"Okay I'm lost; I don't get what is going on?"

Another little chuckle that lacked amusement sounded from the disk around the thing's neck. "You see, little girl, your people, a long time ago, came into our system and took over the land mass on one of our planets, but we wiped them out and then found that this group was not the only one that came out to the stars. So one by one, we found planets with the monkeys on them and we rolled them up and returned them to what they once were. We were about to figure out where your home world was when we lost some cowardly monkeys that escaped our fighters and we have been searching in vain since then.

"Uhm, why do you keep calling us monkeys? We are humans, not apes."

"YOU ARE DESCENDANT FROM THE MONKEYS AND SHOULD HAVE STAYED IN YOUR TREES WHERE YOU BELONGED!"

"Uhm okay, chill out, big guy, just asking, but what's with this star map you're talking about?"

"The star map is what Jim was supposed to find, it tells us where your home world is. Your parents, little girl, were supposed to have it on them, but when we captured them it was not with them, so they must have given it to you."

"YOU KILLED MY PARENTS? YOU..." I yelled as I tried to launch myself off the couch and at the alien, but was slapped down with ease by one of the tentacles before I even got off the couch.

"No, little one, we have not killed them even though they may wish they were dead by the time the commander gets done with them."

"Where are my parents, you squid-eyed fish?"

The alien looked at me with what I figured was a puzzled look for him then laughed out loud as if he thought I had told the funniest joke of all time. "I see that you are so much like your parents, so brave for monkeys. It will be a shame to have to kill you for my people do respect bravery."

I had been trying through this whole conversation to keep the alien's attention on me so that he would not notice the little sounds coming from the back room where my cousin had gone. As we talked, I had been inching my hand closer to the blaster on my side that, unfortunately, had slid under me when I had been first slapped onto the couch.

Just then my cousin made her appearance from the back room, shouting her discovery of my uncle's hidden loot. Rose froze in her tracks looking at the bug-eyed monster standing above me as those dead eyes locked in on her.

I stood up on the couch and drew the blaster from my holster, holding it in two hands and reached out and pulled the trigger just as those eyes turned back to me. The blast sent me over the couch and I landed on my backpack once again knocking the wind out of me.

As I rolled from my pack and stood up, I heard another

blast go off behind me and felt the heat from the energy pass my head. "HEY, I'm on your side, Rose," I said as I looked back at my cousin who was leaning on the side of the doorway holding her own blaster in both her hands.

"What was that, Cassie?"

"That, my dear cousin, was what the dead Jolly would call an alien. Now keep that blaster aimed at the couch while I see if we got it," I said as I slowly moved around the couch to look at what damage, if any, we had done to the alien.

"Is it dead?"

"Yeah, Rose I think you could say that," I said as I looked at what was left of the alien's head. There was one hole right between the eyes where I had shot him and another where the disk that allowed it to talk had resided.

Whoa, I thought, didn't know a blaster would do that kind of damage as I looked down at the weapon at my side. That's when I noticed that the blaster was set for max power and reminded myself that we both needed to change power packs before we left the house and reset the settings also.

"Whoa, cool they have silver blood," Rose said as she moved over to where she could also see the damage we had done to the alien.

I looked down at the mess we had created and the thought did flash through me that it was pretty cool in a way, but the situation we were in came back and slapped me in the face – back to reality.

"Yeah, cool, but we need to get our stuff together and get out of here right now before we encounter any more of these things or anyone else for that matter."

"Yeah, you're right, Cassie, I got the money, and here is your pack," Rose said as she stuffed half of the credits in my pack and the other half in hers.

"Okay, then let's go," I said as I headed toward the door.

"Uhm, Cassie what are we going to do about this thing?" Rose asked as she gave the body of the alien lying on the floor a small kick.

"I don't know? What should we do with it?"

"Well, can the ghost downstairs be hurt if something happens to the house?"

"Of course not, Rose, he is a ghost after all."

"Okay well then don't be mad, but I think maybe we should burn down the house then."

I started to object to the notion of destroying my only home on this planet but then stopped as the thought that most likely I wasn't coming back here anyways crossed my mind as Rose kept on pleading her case in my silence. "Listen, Cassie, I know this is home to you, but if we burn it, it will be awhile before they figure out we aren't here, right"

"Yeah, you're right Rose, don't worry I'm not mad at you. You grab my pack and get the ground car going and take it to the edge of the clearing and I will take care of this."

"Are you sure, Cassie?"

"Yeah, now let's move, girl, before we have any more visitors." And with that Rose grabbed my pack and moved out the door.

On the Run

Once I heard the ground car move I went over to the door of my parent's workshop and reached down to the floorboards and hit a small switch that was made to look like a discoloration in the wood. The switch popped open a panel about eye level and I looked into the room.

"HEY JOLLY! YOU THERE? THIS IS IMPORTANT," I yelled to the ghost that resided in the workshop.

A pale face popped into view in front of the panel taking five years off my young life. I heard a small chuckle as I jumped back from the opening. "No need to shout, little girl, I'm here."

Why is it everyone seems to enjoy calling me little girl? I mean granted I am only five three in my stocking feet, but this was getting really trying fast, I thought. "Listen Jolly my parents were right, the aliens are here and to give us some time I need to burn the place down. That won't, uhm, you know affect you will it?"

Jolly looked at me and smiled. "No, Cassie, it won't affect me even though I shall miss the company that you have given me."

"Uhm thanks, Jolly," I said as I looked at the ghost that I had known all my life. I was stunned for in all that time he had never addressed me as anything but little girl before. "I'll miss you too, Jolly."

I started to turn away when Jolly's gruff voice stopped me once more. "Oh, and little girl you see one of those aliens you get one for me will you?" he said as he moved through the door into the living room.

I looked back behind me at the mess that littered the floor and turned back to Jolly with a big smile. "Already got one for you, Jolly. What is left of him is on my living room floor, and how can you be out here? I thought you were stuck in that room."

Jolly's smile got bigger than before if that was possible. "No, I gave you the privacy you needed, but since you aren't going to be here anymore I can move around, now then, little girl, get on your way and stop wasting time talking to me."

Jolly was right and I moved over to the desk where the com center was and opened a drawer in a cabinet beside it when Rose came back into the house. "Come on, Cassie, we need to move."

"Be right there," I said as I reached in and pulled out two

bottles of oil that my parents used for the emergency lamps needed when we lost power from winter storms. I handed the two bottles over to Rose and told her to spread them around the living room as I went into the kitchen.

I opened three large gas canisters that my parents had used in field cooking and then headed back to the living room. As I got there, I looked at the body on the floor and could see a pale green figure floating above it. Great, I thought, not only do I see human ghosts I get the pleasure of seeing alien ghosts.

"Hey, Cassie, come on. Wake up," Rose said as she shook my arm.

"Yeah, sorry, let's go," I said once more looking at the ghost and seeing it stare back at me with those dead black eyes. The thought flickered across my mind that those eyes were even creepier dead than they were alive. Then I looked over at Jolly who made a shooing motion with his hands before he disappeared.

We went out the door onto the porch when it hit me that I should have grabbed some matches from the kitchen while I was in there. I took a step forward to go back in when Rose grabbed my arm and then handed me a long black round tube with her other hand.

"Need one of these, cousin?"

I looked down at the flare in her hand and grinned, Rose was always more prepared for things than I was. "Yeah, thanks," I said as I took the flare and uncapped it. "Now get to the ground car, 'cause I don't know what is going to happen once I throw this in the house."

I saw Rose run to the end of the clearing and get in the ground car as I struck the end cap against the flare. The flare lit up a bright yellow and as I threw it into the living room and slammed the front door shut. I turned and ran for the ground car as fast as my legs could carry me.

I guess I should have run faster as I was about five feet away from the car when the night was lit up behind me. Then it felt like a large hand lifted me into the air and slammed me into the side of the ground car. As I rolled over and tried to stand, I could hear from far away a voice that sounded like my cousin, Rose, yell my name and then all went black.

The uneven movement of my bed and the drum of the rain woke me up from my sleep and it took me a few seconds to remember where I was. Slowly opening my eyes to the semi-dark sky, I could see that it was early morning, and as dreary of a day as any other on Ecstasy.

"Well, well I see you're awake, cousin," Rose's voice sounded from my left.

"Yeah, how long was I out?" I asked sitting up, not in my bed, but in the seat of the ground car looking out at the rain-soaked landscape around us.

"A couple of hours, Cassie; not too long, how are you feeling?"

I sat up a little straighter in my seat trying to take stock of all the aches and bruises that seemed to cover my body. "Well, I think I'm in one piece, even though I feel like I have gone ten rounds with someone a whole lot bigger than me."

"Yeah, well, cousin, you look like it," Rose said, handing me a small mirror.

I looked in the mirror and saw that I was black and blue along one side of my face and that I had a small trickle of dried blood along my hair line. I touched my head and felt a large knot at the top of my head and winced at the gentle contact.

"You do know, Cassie, when you start a fire you don't do it halfway," Rose said with a snarky smile.

"Yeah, thanks, I think. How about you? Are you okay?"

"I'm fine. I was in the ground car when the house went up in a ball of flames, so I didn't get the full effect. Uhm, what did you do in the kitchen by the way, because I know that two small bottles of lamp oil wouldn't make a house go boom like that?"

I thought back to my trip into the kitchen and then as my head cleared, I smiled back at my cousin. "Uhm I opened three gas canisters."

Rose smiled back. "Yeah, that would do it alright; you always did overdo it, cousin."

I settled back into the ground car's seat and looked around again at the surrounding countryside. "Uhm, Rose where are we? I thought we were headed to the port, right?"

"Don't worry, Cassie. That is where we are headed; I took a short cut on some back roads that my dad knew."

"Back roads?"

"Yeah, my dad and some of his buddies decided that they needed to move from the port and the towns around it to Sanity, the main town, without a lot of nosey people checking what they were transporting."

"I'm sorry, Rose."

"What for, Cassie?"

"Well that you had it so rough with your dad and all and that my parents should have done something more to help you."

Rose was quiet for awhile as she thought this over. "Well, look at it this way, Cassie, if your parents had taken me in then we wouldn't know about these roads or the right people at the port who could get us across to the Teki Reservation now, would we?"

"I guess not Rose, but still?"

"Don't worry about it Cassie, we may have bigger problems and it is why I took these roads in the first place."

"Now what is it?"

"Well after we left the house, I saw some ground cars from the sheriff's come speeding past us."

"That was fast, especially for the law around here," I said as I sat up and looked behind us. The law on Ecstasy moved slowly. Of course, they weren't known for their intelligence either.

"Yeah, that is what I thought too especially when I saw that Preacher was in the lead car headed out to your house. Cassie, do you think that Preacher is one of the aliens?"

I thought back to what I had overheard and seen the other night and now knew what that niggling little feeling had been earlier. "Oh yeah, Rose, in fact, I think Preacher is the big boss of the aliens and we should stay out of his way as much as possible."

"Well, that's why we are on the back roads like this, Cassie."

"Okay sounds like a great plan, but how far can we trust these other guys your dad knew. I mean are they all like him, or I guess I should say like he used to be?"

Rose shook her head at my question and turned a smile my way. "No, most of these guys are pretty good people, Cassie, some may be a little rough around the edges, but for the most part, my dad was real careful on how he treated me around them."

We drove along in a comfortable silence, the two of us getting lost within ourselves during the drive as we watched the daylight, such as it is on this planet, come and grace us with its presence. Pretty soon Rose turned down a small tree lined road that was even skinnier than the one we had been traveling on.

Rose stopped the ground car and pulled out a small red scrap of material from her pack and tied it low around a small branch of one of the trees that sat at the edge of the road, and then hopped back in the ground car and started up again.

"Uhm Rose, what was that for? You know, the red thingy you put on the tree?"

"Oh, just a marker. Nothing to worry about, Cassie."

As we moved down the road, the trees grew closer on each side of us creating almost a tunnel of green that darkened the day even more than usual, but seemed to shelter us from the rain that poured from the sky.

After about fifteen minutes of traveling this road, my curiosity got the better of me. "Uhm Rose, is this another way to the port?"

"No we are close, but I figured that it would be better to hit the port at night. This place we are going to is sort of a rest stop for the people that travel these roads. We will be there soon, Cassie. Don't worry; I know what I'm doing."

"Seems like, cousin, that you have had more experience at this kind of thing than I gave you credit for."

Rose aimed a strange smile my way. "Ever since my mom disappeared I have been plotting a way to get away from my dad. The only problem is that no matter where I went on this planet they would have sent me back to him, so I knew that I only had one chance at this, Cassie."

It was quiet in the car after that and soon I could see that the trees opened up into a small clearing. Rose drove the ground car across the clearing and parked in a small space next to a prefab hut like my parents used out in the field.

"Okay, we're here," Rose said with some satisfaction in her voice.

"And we are where exactly?" I asked looking around at the prefab hut that had been painted to match the surrounding foliage so that unless you knew what you were looking for it would be almost impossible to find.

"Like I said this is a rest stop for certain people. That little marker I put out will let anyone traveling this road know that this one is in use and go to the next one."

"Oh well, I guess that is nice of them."

"Yeah, if we had seen a red marker then we would have had to move on too, but I think maybe I would have taken a chance and seen if we couldn't have gotten help from some of the people around here."

"Do you think these people would have really helped us, Rose?"

Rose stood there and thought about it for a few minutes before answering me. "Maybe, depends on who would have been here. Now come on let's get out of this weather and get some rest," she said as she grabbed up her pack and headed into the hut next to the car.

I grabbed my stuff and followed her over to the hut and was surprised that she walked right into the place without bothering to unlock the door. Rose must have caught the look on my face as she laughed out loud as I followed her into the small building.

"The people that may need this building usually need it in a hurry so it's never locked, and if someone else comes and ransacks it they better not ever meet up with the owners of these rest stops."

"Oh okay, I'll try to remember that, cousin," I said looking out the window once more, expecting to see a horde of angry owners come storming out of the trees any second.

"Don't worry, Cassie, we're as safe as we can be here, so relax and let's get some breakfast and then some sleep, okay?"

I yawned at the mention of sleep, but my stomach won out when it let out a large growl at the mention of food. We dug into our packs and pulled out some field rations and

Rose started to heat them up on a tiny little stove unit.

As she was cooking, I looked over the hut that we were using noticing that even for being out in the middle of nowhere it was kept quite clean. One wall had four bunks lined up end to end with thick blankets rolled at each end of a bed.

I walked to a small door opposite the front door and opened it to find a sanitary room that held the basic necessities along with shelves that were lined with numerous types of first aid kits. As I closed the door to the sanitary room, the smell of food caused me to drift over to where Rose was cooking our breakfast.

"Smells good," I said.

"That's good, for it's done," Rose said as she moved over to the table and dumped half of the skillet on my plate and half on hers.

I sat down at the table, my stomach protesting the lack of food as I scooped up the first mouthful and stuffed it in. "It tastes great," I said as the hot food slid down to meet my empty stomach.

"Good, I was a little worried since you can do only so much with field rations," she said as she set a glass of water down in front of both our spots at the table.

Yeah, well, if Rose hadn't been with me I would have been out in the cold and eating cold rations. I certainly wasn't going to complain about her cooking. We ate in silence with the both of us fighting to keep our eyes open as our bellies filled with the food before us.

Pretty soon we were both done and Rose and I cleaned up the mess in the hut and we each headed for our own bunks. "Think one of us should keep an eye out, Rose?" I asked as I rolled the blankets out over the bunk bed I had chosen.

"No, don't worry Cassie, like I said we should be safe here," Rose said, her voice sounding softer as sleep took her down into its embrace. My own eyes soon closed as well and I followed my cousin down into sleep's sweet dreams.

Unexpected Help

I don't know if it was the delicious smell of Rose's cooking that woke me from my deep sleep or the subdued voices that were talking in the hut. As the thought crossed my sleep induced brain that there should only be one voice, that of my cousin's, I quickly sat up in bed and looked over toward the cooking area.

"Uhh, she wakes, Rose," a deep gruff voice sounded from the table that we had used earlier in the day.

"Uhm Rose, who is this?" I asked my cousin as I looked at the large bear of a man that was sitting down at the table giving me the same scrutiny that I was giving him.

"Cassie, this is Moe, Moe this is Cassie, my cousin," Rose said as she emptied a huge pile of food on three plates that were now sitting on the table.

"How you doing, Cassie?" the big man said as he dug into the pile of food in front of him.

I looked over at the man and then back to Rose with the

obvious question written on my face, but my cousin shrugged her shoulders, and sat down and started to dig into her own plate of food.

"You going to come and eat some of this food or can I have your share?" Moe asked with an expectant look at me and then at my plate.

I hopped out of bed as the smell of the food drew me toward the table and I sat down and started to shovel my portion into my mouth as fast as I could. I had to smile at the look of disappointment on Moe's face as he watched my dinner disappear. I mean I may be small, but that doesn't mean I can't put away my share of the grub when it comes down to it.

"Well for such a little thing you can put it away at least," Moe said with his own smile echoing my thoughts.

Once again the only sound was the sound of eating and silverware scraping the last scraps of food off the plates in front of us. Once we were done with our meal, Rose and I cleaned up the area leaving Moe sitting at the table in quiet thought.

"That was even better than this morning's meal," I said as Rose and I came back to the table and sat down.

"Yeah, well it was better because Moe said I could use the supplies here," Rose said.

I turned toward Moe and put on my most sincere smile and thanked him for the meal, but all this did was get a large grunt from the man. I wasn't sure if that was thanks or what so I ignored it for now.

"Okay, now that we're all fed and the pleasantries are over how about you girls tell me why the law is so hell bent on getting their hands on you and why I shouldn't turn you into them," Moe said looking between the two of us.

Both of us jumped up from the table and reached for our blasters that were supposed to be hanging in their holsters at our sides, but each of us came up empty-handed.

"Looking for these, girls?" Moe said as he held up our weapons in his hand. The way he held them, they looked like tiny toys in his hand.

"Moe, I thought you were one of the good ones?" my cousin whispered as she looked at the two weapons we really needed, for we weren't going against Moe without them.

Moe looked at the two of us and then smiled as he threw the two blasters onto the table and leaned back into his chair. "Oh I am one of the good ones, kid, I wanted to prove it to you and so I came in here and liberated these toys from you before I woke you up. Now sit down and talk to me."

Rose moved over to the table and sat, carefully picking up her weapon and checking that the power pack was in it and fully charged. While I walked over and grabbed mine and pointed it at Moe.

"Are you one of them?" I asked

Moe looked at me puzzled for a few seconds. "One of who, kid?"

I stared at Moe trying to figure out if he was putting on an act, or really confused over two girls out in the woods all on their own.

"Cassie, if he was one of the aliens I don't think we would still be here, do you?" Rose said as she looked up at me from her seat.

I figured that my cousin was right in that if Moe was one of the aliens he had plenty of time to take care of us. I mean it's not like anyone would have heard us out here in the middle of nowhere if Moe had meant us harm.

"Okay, you're right, Rose," I said as I sat down at the table next to my cousin, but I left the blaster on the table never far from my hand, just in case.

"Okay girls, what is this alien bull you seem to be peddling?" Moe asked as the silence in the hut lingered on for a few minutes.

Rose and I looked at each other for a few minutes before we decided to explain to him all that we had been through and what we knew about the star map and ship. I figured that Moe would get up and leave or least call us crazy, but he sat throughout the whole explanation in silence.

"So that's why Jim was acting so strange lately," Moe said

after our tale.

"That's all you have to say after we tell you about a map and ship and aliens? No questions about any of that stuff at all?" I said as I eyed the big man.

"Listen, kid, some of us are not as backward as most of the hicks on this rock, and some of us have kept a long history of what happened and why we are on this planet. That's why your parents contacted us to get them across to the Teki Reservation to find this ship and the map."

"Oh," was all that squeaked out of the two of us as we looked at the man before us.

"So you know where my parents are then?" I asked, hope briefly flaring in my chest before Moe squashed it with his next words.

"No, sorry; the man that we sent with your parents never made it back so we didn't have any idea what had happened to them until we heard that they had been killed," Moe said, with the sympathy for my plight written all over his face.

"My parents aren't dead, at least not yet," I said.

"And you know this how, kid?"

"I know this because just before Rose and I killed an alien, he told me."

"You two little kids killed an alien all by yourselves?" Moe asked the look of disbelief written all over his face would have been funny if not for the seriousness of the situation.

"Yeah, we did Moe," my cousin said.

"Okay and then how did you two little things kill an alien?"

"Easy, we used these two little toys, as you called them, at full power," I said as I held up the small blaster in my hand.

"Yeah, I guess those would do the trick at full power alright," Moe said with a whistle.

"So are you going to help us or turn us over to the law?" I asked.

"First, what are your plans right now, girls?"

"Well we figured that we would get over to the reservation and find the ship and then rescue my parents from the aliens, what else can we do?"

"Good plan, so how about we head out to the port so we can figure out where this ship is," Moe said as he raised his large bulk from his chair and headed to the door.

"Uhm Moe, we know where the ship is, or at least we have a pretty good idea where it is with the map we have," Rose said then as she realized what she had said she slapped her hand over her mouth and whispered to me, "Sorry."

"No problem, cousin," I said as I moved from the table and pointed the blaster in my hand once more at Moe. "And just what makes you think that you are coming with us, Moe?"

"I'm coming with you," Moe said as his hand snaked out and grabbed the blaster out of my hand and pointed it at my cousin. "Because you two need help on this little trip," he finished as he turned the blaster and handed the weapon back to me.

"Oh yeah, I see," I said as I took the blaster from his hand. "So you're going with us right now huh?"

Once again we were on the road, except this time we were riding in Moc's ground car. It had been specially modified to carry cargo and had a few other little options that Moe built in himself. As I rode behind the two front seats, I sat perched on a ledge with my legs dangling down into an open hole that leads to where the engine compartment of this vehicle was supposed to be.

"Nice hiding place you got here, Moe," I said looking down at the cramped space below my feet.

"Yeah, had to do some modifications so I could have some space for my special cargo," Moe said with a grin.

"You really think I will fit in this small space?"

"You're small, kid, so yeah, you should fit alright if need be. It's either that or the law gets you, take your pick."

"You have to forgive Cassie, Moe, she doesn't like small enclosed spaces all that much ever since we were kids and she 'accidentally' got locked into a small cabinet playing hide and seek with me," Rose said with a chuckle.

I looked daggers over at my cousin and the smile she threw my way. "I always wondered if you were the one that locked me in there, cousin."

"Who me? Now, why would I do such a thing as that? Oh yeah, right, maybe because someone threw a handful of shock worms into the shower that I was in," Rose said with a frown.

I gave a small laugh at the image of Rose dancing in the shower as the small worms gave off their little electric charges in the water that had pooled in the wash basin. Not enough to hurt a person, but it was definitely enough of a charge that it woke you up I the morning. "Oh yeah, now I remember," I said.

We both looked at each other and then broke out laughing at the antics that had gotten us grounded that summer by my parents. Moe looked between the two of us and shook his head, saying something about how it was good that he didn't have kids.

It got quiet again as we ate up some more of the road that would take us to the port and hopefully over to where the ship and my momma and daddy were. As the night wore on my eyes closed and my head nodded up and down from the rocking motion of the ground car. Even with all the sleep we had gotten during the day, I found myself dozing.

After bumping my head on the back window one time too many, I asked Moe if this thing had a com unit thinking maybe some music or news would keep me awake. Moe looked back at me with one eyebrow raised as if to say really, and then he turned forward and flipped a switch on the car's dash.

The music and news that came out of our one main town on this planet wasn't much, but it kept those of us out in the boonies informed enough about what was going on in our world such as it was.

A static filled song was finishing up and it was quiet for a few seconds until a new voice filled the air.

"And now important news. All citizens are to be on the lookout for two girls on the run. They are wanted for questioning in the disappearance of two men. These two girls could be dangerous and are not to be approached on your own. If you see these two girls, contact the sheriff's office. One girl is described as being five foot. . ."

Moe reached over and flipped the switch off on the com unit and glanced over at Rose and then back at me before focusing back on the road. "That, my friend, is why you may need to hide and why we disguised your cousin, Cassie."

I looked over at my cousin who now had her hair cut so short that I could see her scalp through her blond stubble. Moe had given her some clothes that when on her lean tall figure made her more look more like a boy than the girl she was.

"Well, why not disguise me too?" I asked.

"Because, kid, your cousin here can pull it off, but with your figure it would be a little harder to disguise you as a guy."

I glanced down at myself and had to agree somewhat with Moe's statement I guess, even though I was short, momma always did say that I had filled out nice where it counted.

"Besides they are going to be looking for two of you, if we get stopped they are more likely not going to look too closely at your cousin if she is alone with me, but if there are two kids along with me they are going to examine them real close-like. Whoever is running the show doesn't seem to be as stupid as the usual law is around here," Moe said.

"Do you think maybe these aliens have taken over the law too, Moe?" Rose whispered.

"Yeah, could be, Rose. It would explain why they have gotten so efficient in cutting down the trade routes around here like they have. I've had some good men disappear lately."

"Listen, Moe, you said before that you weren't surprised about the aliens and that you knew about why we were on this planet, why is that?" I asked.

Moe glanced into the mirror above him and caught my

reflection in it before answering me. "Well, kid, when we came to this planet there was some crew that survived the crash, but most of the survivors were people that we took on from the last planet. When the Captain was killed, his pregnant wife took over command of the crew and anyone that would follow her."

"And the rest of them?" Rose asked.

"The rest of the people were pretty worthless. When we first got down on the planet you know we landed on the Teki's Reservation. Well from all accounts they were ready to help us and all would have been fine if some of those worthless ones hadn't caused a ruckus. No one knows what exactly happened anymore, but if it hadn't been for the quick thinking of the Captain's wife, all of the castaways would have been killed."

"Smart woman," I said.

"Yes she was, and from what I gathered from your parents, you're like her in looks and spirit, Cassie."

"Me?"

"Yeah, you, didn't your parents ever tell you that your mom was a descendant of the Captain's wife."

"Uhm no," I whispered.

Moe chuckled at my quiet voice. "Yeah, well I have seen some old pictures of her and you could pass for a spitting image of the old gal, size and all."

"So then what?" Rose asked Moe.

"Oh sorry, after the Captain's wife led the group over here, the castaways settled down and tried to make a life out of this rock. Those of us that were once crew members knew that sooner or later that the aliens would probably find us; we kept an eye out for anything unusual happening on this planet. After awhile the others forgot what happened in the past, we never did."

"What was the Captain's wife's name anyways?" I asked, curious about one of my ancestors.

Moe smiled at me again. "Like I said, you have a lot in common for her name was Cassie like you, in fact, your mother named you after her from what I understand."

"Well I see that Cassie was the Captain's wife and all, but why would the crew follow her? I mean she wasn't anyone that important was she?" Rose asked a questioning look on her face.

"Yeah, well you see Cassie was the Captain's wife alright, but before that she was the second in command of the ship that they were on. The Captain and his wife were in love for a long time, so when they were ready to retire they got quietly hitched and had a baby. Once the service found this out, they kicked out his wife and were going to do the same to the captain when all the trouble started to happen on the outer rim worlds."

"So that's why the crew followed her."

"Oh yeah, like I said Cassie was hell on wheels even more than the captain. From what I understand he was the quieter of the two, but that is usually what happens between a captain and their XO."

"And the crew?" I asked.

"Well, the crew drifted away from the town. Most of the people around the port and the independents are from the crew. In fact, the port was built with the idea in mind to make contact with the Tekis and as an escape in case, the aliens finally found us."

"How about this ship we heard about?" I asked.

"Well, it took us a long time before the Teki would trust us again, so that the exact location of the ship was lost over time, but finally we made contact with some Teki that seemed to be friendly and ready to forget old grievances."

"But I was told that it was the Tekis that killed my parents."

"Yeah, that's what we were told too, but I have a feeling that that was a setup and it was aliens that wanted to get a hold of your parents, because of the star maps that the scout ships held within their data banks."

"What star maps?"

"Why, the star maps that lead right back to our home world, what else?" Moe said.

"Oh, this is getting too complicated for two girls who knew nothing about aliens, or ships or any of this stuff just a few nights ago," Rose said with a sigh.

"So you saying you're ready to give up on finding the ship or Cassie's parents?" Moe asked.

"No one is giving up on this little quest of ours, right Rose?"

"Yeah, you're right Cassie, anyways if there are aliens on this planet then we need to get off it as soon as possible, because from what we have heard they don't leave anyone alive behind."

"Well changing the subject Moe, how long until we get to the port and I have to hide?" I asked looking down once more at the tiny, dark space that my legs dangled in.

Moe motioned to the front of the ground car with his head and grunted. Rose and I looked out the front of the window and saw the low glow of lights that bounced off of the clouds before us trying to fight through the black night and heavy rain that was pounding the roof of the car.

Big Booms in the Night

About fifteen minutes later, Moe pulled the ground car over to the side of the road and turned to me. "Alright listen to me closely, girly, because all our lives depend on you being very quiet for the next hour or so."

"AN HOUR!" I said looking down at the hole and shaking my head at the big man.

"Now quiet, kid, and listen," Moe said grabbing my arm and pulling me so close that we were now eye to eye. "Any girl that can kill an alien should be able to handle a little time in a spacious hiding place like this," Moe said now sweeping his hand at the hole below me.

"Yeah, well if it's so spacious, how about you crawl into it and I'll drive the ground car?"

Moe chuckled and looked down at the hole and then back at me. "We already talked about this, kid; if you want to find this ship and your parents then we need to get you into the port without being seen. Now, just around the bend, this road turns into the main lane that leads to the port. Then it's a quick ten-minute drive to the port gates, and another ten minutes to my boat if all goes well."

"And if it all goes to hell, then what?" I asked.

Moe glanced at Rose then me and smiled an evil smile I never wanted to be directed at me again. "Well then if all goes to hell then we take as many of them with us as we can. So I would suggest that you girls have your weapons ready, but don't use them until I tell you to, understand me?"

We both nodded at Moe and loosened our blasters in their holsters. "How about you, Moe? You got a weapon on you?" Rose asked with some concern.

Moe gave each of us that smile again that cooled my blood. "Yeah, I have this," Moe said releasing my arm and sitting back in his seat, and pulling out a knife that would be big enough for a small sword for anyone else.

"Oh yeah, that should do I guess," Rose said looking at the knife with eyes that I was sure was as wide as my own.

"Of course if there are a lot of them then I can always break out old Betsy here," Moe said as he tapped the front of the dash and a compartment opened showing off a crossbow that had a large round barrel attached to the bottom of it.

"Uhm Moe, you think an arrow will take out an alien?" I asked, now sure that Moe wasn't quite all there.

Moe chuckled, "Oh don't you worry your pretty little head off, girly. One of these bolts hits anything, and they will need a sponge to pick up what's left of them."

We both looked at Moe, the puzzlement obvious on both our faces. "Explosive heads, kids," Moe said with another deep chuckle.

"Oh yeah, that would do it too Moe. Remind me to never make you mad at me, okay?" I said with a smile.

"Yeah, me too Moe, I'm glad you're on our side."

Moe laughed and laughed then stopped as suddenly as he started as he pushed me down into the hole. "Time to get going, kid, so down you go, and remember no matter what stay down there quiet, not a peep out of you," Moe said as he slid the cover of the hole over my head.

The darkness encircled me as Moe closed the top of his hiding place and I heard the click of the door latch. I curled up in the dark hole, my legs touching my chest with my head ducked down between my knees. I hoped that if Moe had ever tried to hide someone else in this spot that they were as small as me. Then as the ground car started up once again, I stretched out a little in the dark and found that the hole was a little bigger than it looked. Yeah, I know guess being short does have some perks.

I leaned back and found that I could push my legs out a little and that, in this position, I could raise my head up from the cramped pose I had started in when I crawled in the hole; but still this was not going to be the most comfortable ride I had ever made in a ground car. I reached down and slowly lifted my blaster from its holster and held it in my hands, feeling a little more comfortable with my weapon ready.

After what seemed like forever, I felt the ground car come to a stop. Moe told me that for the most part that the area I was hiding in was soundproof and the engine noise would kill any other sounds, but it would have been nice to know what was happening out there.

The ground car seemed to sit for a long time until I felt it rock as though someone had jumped in the back. Then I could feel the vehicle shift from side to side as though something was being shifted around in the bed of the car.

The silence that ensued after that was driving me crazy and my imagination was working overtime. All I could think of was that both my cousin and Moe were either captured or dead and that a swarm of aliens were even now surrounding the ground car to take me to some place I know I didn't want to go to.

I almost wet myself when I felt the ground car once more rock as someone got into the front and it started moving. We seemed to be moving at a snail's pace forever when the ground car came to a stop, and the engine shut off.

The silence seemed to last forever until I heard someone fumble with the cover of the hole I was in. I pointed the blaster I had at the opening and vowed that I would take out as many of these creatures as I could before they got me.

As the cover opened and I pressed my fingers back on the trigger, it registered that it was Moe's smiling face that was looking back down at me. "I hope you aren't going to shoot me, kid?" Moe said looking down the barrel of the weapon I held in my hands.

"Sorry, been so long I thought something had happened to the two of you."

"So expecting maybe an alien or something, girl?" Moe said with a chuckle.

"Yeah, something like that, Moe."

"Well don't worry, we got by the gate at the port, and we are almost down to my boat, so I'll keep this open, but peek your head out and nothing more and be ready to duck down fast if need be, okay?"

"Yeah, Moe thanks, I need some air after being down there so long," I said as I adjusted my body so that I was kneeling just enough to stick my head above the edge of the hole I had been hiding in.

"Uhm Cassie, you weren't down there that long," Rose said as she looked back and down at me.

"Seemed like an hour or more to me, cousin. Like I said, I was really starting to get worried about the two of you."

"Well we hit a little snarl of traffic at the gate since they were checking everyone going in and out, but you were only down there about twenty-five minutes tops, Cassie."

"God, I hate dark, small places," I said to the laughter of the two in the front seat.

We drove through the port area, heading for the water and Moe's boat. For the most part, the streets of the port were dark and quiet since most of the folks around here were up early and went to bed as soon as it was dark out.

Once we hit an area that was lit up, Moe glanced back at me and whispered that we were near some warehouses and I needed to make sure that I wasn't seen so I ducked down until just my eyes were above the lip of my hiding place.

Once we were past this point, we were once again in a darkened area and I could now smell the water even through the closed windows of the ground car. "Okay, you can come out of there now, Cassie," Moe said as we moved along a road that followed the water.

Another five or ten-minute drive and we came upon a small marina that had two docks stretching out to the water like two seeking fingers. Along each side of the wooden docks, boats of all sizes and shapes were lined up like soldiers waiting for their orders to go out onto the field and march.

"Which one is yours?' I asked as Moe pulled his ground car to the side of one of the docks.

"My baby is at the end of the docks, let's get your stuff and get on the boat so that we can get out of here, okay?" Moe said looking over his shoulder at the port gate that we could see far in the distance.

"Yeah, sure is everything alright, Moe?" Rose asked.

"Yeah, I guess it just seemed like some of those guys I knew at the gate were a little off, sort of like they weren't themselves," Moe said with a frown.

"I know what you mean, Moe," Rose said with an equal frown. "It sort of reminded me of how Jade acted last time I saw him."

Then it hit me that Rose hadn't seen the alien that we had killed in its former form. "Uhm, you guys, that was an alien disguised as Jade that we killed at the house."

"Really? Are you sure?" Rose asked.

"Yeah, when he came in the house he was Jade and then he shimmered and he turned into an alien. So yeah, I'm pretty sure that that wasn't Jade."

"Oh damn, so those guys weren't the guys I knew then?"

Moe asked.

"No, and if they were aliens then that most likely means that the guys you knew are dead because the alien told me that they don't keep anyone around when they take their form," I explained to the two of them.

"Okay, I like this less and less so let's get you two on the boat and get going out to sea," Moe said as he as he grabbed his pack and Betsy out of the ground car.

Then I glanced over at the gates of the port and I could see several vehicles with lights flashing pull up to them. A few seconds later lights lit up the night sky and sirens started to sound, filling the area with their constant wail.

"Come on, girls, run now," Moe said as he headed down the dock at a trot that ate up space quickly.

We both froze for a second and then Rose and I were headed out after Moe, our feet pounding on the wooden boards of the dock echoing in the night, underscored by the screaming sirens at the gate.

All three of us ran as fast as we could, with Rose soon catching up to Moe with those long lean legs of hers. If she knew where Moe's boat was she probably would have run past him and beat him to our destination.

As usual, with my short legs, I was bringing up the rear and I kept glancing back watching the ground cars from the gate follow the same route we had. I knew that as fast as they were moving down the road that they would not take nearly as long as we had to get down to the dock.

Even though I was at a dead run, I couldn't help but notice all the beautiful sailing ships that we passed as we ran down the dock. As we passed each one, I could see the sleek lines and tall masts as we passed them. I couldn't wait to see Moe's baby as he called her and was surprised when Rose and Moe stopped at the end of the dock for there was no ship there that I could see.

I stopped next to the two of them as I saw my cousin turn and start to climb down the ladder into the darkness below. "Uhm Moe, where's your boat?" I said looking back at the ground cars that were now closing fast on the dock area.

"What are you talking about?" Moe said as he looked behind us out to the road and then down into the darkness before shouting, "Gus, James, get this tub revved up, weapons manned —we're leaving now."

I looked down once again after I glanced back at the road and saw that the vehicles were almost up to the ground car we had abandoned at the end of the dock.

"Let's go, kid, you're next," Moe said pushing me toward the ladder.

"Where?" I said as the night was suddenly lit up by some

low red lights from below. I gasped as I looked down at the low-slung craft that lay at the base of the ladder. "You want me to get on that small thing and go out there?" I said pointing down first at the boat and then out at the dark water that was lapping at the dock and boat below me.

"Kid you have a quick choice to make, you either climb down or I throw you down. Made up your mind?" Moe said with a grin.

Well, since he put it that way, I thought, as I threw my pack over my shoulder, turned and started down the ladder to the "boat" below me.

I climbed down the ladder as fast as I could, afraid that I would be knocked off into the water below since Moe was right above me moving at full speed. As my feet hit the metal deck of the boat, I felt two hands grab me from behind and slide me across the deck toward an open hatchway. I stopped short of the hatch turning as I slid so I was now looking back at the dock and Moe who was just now hitting the deck of his baby.

"Gus, you guys ready to go?" Moe asked a small man that stood looking up at Moe. The red lights on the boat made it hard to see exactly what he looked like, but I could hear the laughter in his voice as he answered Moe.

"Yeah, captain, James has the engine revved up and ready to go and I have all weapons loaded and primed.

"Good, then let's get out of here, Gus," Moe said as he

reached into his pocket and took out a small box.

"Right you are, captain," Gus said as he dived for the enclosed cockpit of the boat seconds later. We were pulling from the dock and I could see several dozen men running past the ships that lined the dock while others kneeled down and took shots at us from between the boats.

I dived down into the open hatch of the deck next to me and looked over the edge just as my cousin was when I heard Moe growl, "Oh well what a waste of boats, but they picked the wrong people to mess with." And with that, Moe pressed down on the box in his hand.

As the boat we were on picked up speed and we pulled further away from the dock, I watched first Moe's ground car go up in an explosion of fire and body parts into the night sky; followed then by the boats that lined the dock, one by one.

As the night sky was lit up, I could see that the bodies that were flying in the air did not resemble human bodies so I didn't feel any remorse at seeing the flames that swept the docks from one end to another.

"Oh damn, the poor people on those boats," I heard my cousin whisper as I saw tears shining in her eyes from the light being thrown off from the burning dock and boats.

"No worries, kid. I own all those boats and the dock area, so I made sure there was no one around," Moe said as he walked up and looked down at us.

"Oh well how about the other boats," I said as I watched figures swarm all over the other dock and boats.

"Oh yeah, thanks for reminding me," Moe said as he turned and looked over at the other dock that was receding in the distance. "Gus, you want to take care of this," Moe said looking at the man at the wheel of the boat.

"Yeah, no problem, Captain," the man said as I felt the boat turn in the water so that the front of the boat was now pointed at the dock. As we came around, I saw two small streaks leave the front of the boat and fly over the water until, that is, they impacted the last two boats on the dock.

As the two streaks hit the boats, the engines revved and the boat turned once again out toward open water. As we sped through the water, I could see and hear the explosions of the boats up and down the other dock once again lighting up the night as bright as the day.

Both Rose and I tore our eyes from the destruction that Moe and his people had caused at the docks and looked at the big man that was still standing above us looking down with a big smile on his face. "Well, kids I think I may have taken out more aliens than you have."

"Didn't know that this was a contest," I heard my cousin mumble next to me as she glanced my way.

I don't know if Moe was ignoring my cousin or if he hadn't heard her, but he smiled at us and reached down and grabbed both of us by the back of our collars and hauled us up on the deck from the hatch we had been hiding in. "Come on kids, out of the gunner's pit, and let's get you below where you can catch some shut eye before we hit the Teki's land."

With all the action we had been through I thought that there was no way I would be able to rest, let alone sleep, but as we walked toward the wheelhouse of the boat, I could feel my eyes get heavy with sleep.

Well maybe a little nap wouldn't be such a bad idea, after all, I thought, as we passed the man named Gus who was concentrating on moving the boat through the open water in front of us. Before I went below with my cousin and Moe, I looked at the surrounding night seeing only the darkness that seemed to swallow the land behind us.

Island Hopping

I don't know if it was the slow rocking of the boat that woke me or the smell of freshly cooked food that was wafting from the tiny galley beside us. I opened my eyes and turned over to see Rose once more standing in a cooking area making breakfast.

I really need to talk to my cousin about waking me and not doing all the chores, I thought, as I started to sit up in the bunk and rapped my head on the low ceiling of the bed. Rose turned and smiled at me as I rubbed where my head and the ceiling had connected. Yeah, the ceiling won that round no matter how hard people tell me my head is.

"Hey, sleepy head; good to see you're finally ready to wake up," Rose said.

Then it suddenly hit me that we were stopped dead in the water. I looked at my cousin with some concern, but she once again smiled and shook her head before answering my unasked question. "No we aren't there yet, but from what Moe said we should be there tonight, no problem."

"Then why are we stopped, Rose?"

Rose shrugged her shoulders and turned back to stir whatever smelled so good on the stove. "Moe said he wanted to lay up for the day, just in case."

"In case what?"

"I guess in case someone managed to follow us or came after us later," Rose said as she grabbed a couple of full plates and nodded at the others sitting next to the stove. "Now come on and grab those plates and follow me up topside, Cassie."

After Rose moved out of the way, I rolled out of the bunk and grabbed the other three plates and followed my cousin up the short steps that led to the wheelhouse above. "Well, good morning, kid, glad to see you're finally up," I heard Moe's voice rumble at me as my head appeared through the hatch.

"Yeah, thanks, Moe," I said I as looked around the area where we were stopped. I could see that we had put in at some shoreline for the boat was tied up to some trees that grew right down to the waterline. "Uhm, where are we exactly?"

Moe looked around and smiled. "We're taking the back way into the Teki Reservation."

"The back way?" I questioned. "I didn't know that there was a back way or for that matter a front or a side way to the reservation. I thought you hopped in a boat and went across the water and there you were."

"Yeah, well most people think that way, but for those of us that ply the ocean, we know there is more than one way to get where you are headed. The back side as we call it is dotted with these small islands about one hundred miles out from the Teki's mainland, but the best thing is that once you hit these islands the water gets very shallow."

As Moe was talking, I handed him a plate of food and also the man that he called Gus who was sitting next to him. Taking my own plate, I walked over to the side of the boat that was closest to the water and looked down. I was surprised that I could see the ocean floor in the crystal clear waters and all the small creatures that called these waters home.

Looking up I saw in all directions various sized islands that dotted the horizon. Some of the islands were just small bare rock jutting out of the water, whereas others were large land masses that were covered from one end to the other with all kinds of vegetation.

"Why didn't we head to the Reservation right away? Why come this way, Moe?" I asked as I looked over to the big man.

"We took this way because I knew that no matter how fast we went those people on the mainland would have someone waiting for us before we got close to the reservation. My baby may be fast, but she ain't as fast as some of the patrol ships that the law has out here."

"Well, won't they find us here then?"

"Don't worry, kid. Like I said, they are fast ships but the problem is that they were built for the deep ocean, not the shallow waters around here."

"Oh okay, I guess," I said looking for the first time at the boat that we were on in the light of day. I can't say I was very impressed with the sight of Moe's baby. It was short enough that the five of us could stand side by side with our arms outstretched and we would go from the end of the boat to the front, with it being about eight feet or so across.

Moe must have seen my doubts about his boat written on my face because as he finished his meal he handed me his plate and smiled at me and looked around at his pride and joy. "Don't worry, kid, she don't look like much but she has enough firepower to take on any problems we run into."

"Okay, sure," I said as the other crew members and my cousin handed me their plates one after another.

"Your turn for dishes, kid," Moe said as he jumped off the boat onto the island we were tied up to. "I mean that is only fair since your cousin there made the grub, right?" Moe tossed over his shoulder as the other two crew members also hopped off the boat and all three disappeared into the undergrowth of the island we were attached to.

"Yeah, sure, no problem," I said to the empty spot that the

men had been in just seconds ago.

My cousin laughed at the look on my face and came up to me. "Come on, I'll help you clean up, cousin," Rose said as she grabbed some of the plates out of my hand and headed back down into the small galley.

I lay on the front deck of the boat with Rose, trying to catch the sunlight dappling down through the trees and leaves of this island. Moe and his two companions still hadn't returned from whatever it was they were doing so we were killing time with nothing to do after cleaning the morning's breakfast dishes. The breeze that played through the islands cooled us from the hot muggy cloud filled day that seemed to hover over this area. Gods I was getting so tired of clouds.

It was getting on to night and the lazy day felt good after all the hectic running around we had been doing the last couple of days. Rose and I discussed what we knew about the aliens and everything else we had learned these last couple of days, but the talk died down between us as each of us dozed throughout the day.

My stomach let out a small growl to let me know that it didn't really appreciate me skipping lunch and it was time to be fed. "Hey Rose, let's get some food together for the crew, so they don't think we haven't done anything today,"

I said as I rolled off of my back and shook my cousin's shoulder to wake her.

Sitting up fast and gasping, Rose looked around wild-eyed at me. Don't know if it was the shaking on her shoulder or the sudden crashing that was coming from the island's foliage next to the boat.

Suddenly Moe and Gus jumped out of the bushes as though they were being chased by a herd of demons from hell, both men hitting the deck of the boat with their heavy boots clanking onto the metal and making the boat rock back and forth in the water.

"GUS, YOU GET BELOW AND START THE ENGINES NOW!" Moe bellowed as he headed toward the wheel house of the boat. Gus disappeared as quick as a ghost below decks and I could hear him swearing from his hole.

Both Rose and I scrambled from the front of the boat and hopped down on the deck by the wheelhouse as Moe hit the starter on the engines, revving the power of the boat to its max. "Here kid," Moe said as he handed me a long knife. "Cut the ropes so we can get out of here now!"

"But what about the other guy?" I asked looking over at the bushes and trees of the island we were tied to.

"He ain't coming, now cut the lines if you want to live, kid," Moe said as he grabbed Rose and sat her down at a panel that had what looked like a com screen and joysticks attached to it.

I ran and cut the two ropes that held us to the island and turned toward the front of the boat as I heard a mechanical whir from the front. A set of blasters had popped out of the deck where only minutes ago Rose and I had been resting. They were moving in several directions, side to side and up and down as Rose moved the joysticks in front of her.

As Moe finished talking with her, my cousin reached down and buckled herself into the seat, then looked down at her screen with all her concentration. I stood there looking at my cousin thinking that Moe was setting her up for a com game when he walked up to me and grabbed my arm and led me to the back of the boat.

"What's going on, Moe?" I said as he picked me up and slipped me into a seat in the small hole that Rose and I had hidden in during last night's fireworks.

"Buckle up, kid, for it's going to be a rough ride, then I'll show you what to do," Moe said as he kneeled down next to the hole I was in.

My head and shoulders came above the deck of the boat and in front of me, I saw the same set up with the joysticks sitting in front of me that Rose had. As I buckled the belt and then each shoulder strap, Moe reached down on the panel and hit a green button and out of the back deck popped up a set of blasters identical to the ones in front of the boat. Guess I was wrong, this wasn't a com game – this was real.

"Alright listen to me carefully, kid," Moe said in a calm voice. "Grab a hold of the two joysticks in front of you, but don't press the triggers on the sticks."

I grabbed both joysticks, keeping my fingers away from the red triggers, and watched as the blasters moved side to side as my hands shook from being so nervous.

"Alright good job, kid, now remember move the sticks side to side for the guns to go left and right, and back and forth to go up and down," Moe said and then pointed at the small com screen that had popped up on the edge of the deck that was now lit up with a small round circle and crosshairs. "When your target hits the middle of the crosshairs, pull the triggers. Got that kid?"

"But I thought you said other ships couldn't get to us here, Moe?"

"They're not ships, they're flyers."

"Flyers? We don't have anything that flies on this planet, Moe," I said now totally confused on what was going on here.

"You're right, kid, we don't have anything that flies on this planet, but they do," Moe said as we both looked up at a weird whistling sound that passed over our heads. With us still under the cover of the trees on the island and the twilight that had finally darkened the sky, I couldn't see what had made the noise but, whatever it was, it wasn't human – that I knew.

Moe looked down at me and smiled as he said, "Now we're going to make a run for the mainland and I think there are four of those things up there, so let's see how good of a shot you girls are."

With that, Moe jumped up and headed to the steering wheel of the boat. As I looked back behind me at my cousin, I could see that she was as nervous as I was but she smiled at me and winked before putting her head down to concentrate on the screen before her.

Well, I thought, as I looked out over the com screen and the back of the boat at least with the setup I had I wouldn't have my head buried down looking at the com screen and missing all the action.

I could feel the boat's engines rev as Moe put more power to them and I was wondering what he was waiting for when I heard that strange whistling noise pass over us once more, and then felt the deck under me surge away from the island, the front blaster shooting bright bolts of energy into the air.

In the darkness that had fallen, I caught the faint impression of flat teardrop shapes in the sky, flying and weaving in the air until a burst from the blasters turned one into a flaming star that fell to the water below it.

As I watched the water bubble and boil where the ship had fallen, I heard the sounds of more of the fliers behind us.

Feeling the boat's aft end leave the water from an explosion, I turned back to my own area of responsibility as the back end of the boat slammed back into the water and I was drenched from the wave that washed over me.

"YOU GOING TO SHOOT THEM DOWN, KID, NEXT PASS OR JUST WAVE AS THEY GO BY!" Moe shouted as two ships passed over our boat, my cousin's blaster chasing after the ships, but missing, as they swung around to come up from behind us again.

Watching the two airships moving up at us, I could see that one was coming in low while the other was coming in high, ensuring that I could only get a shot at one of them in this pass. Green streaks of power left the front of both fliers as they approached our boat making the water geyser into the air as each blot hit the ocean.

I pulled the joysticks back and pressed the triggers down while aiming at the higher of the two fliers. I held my breath as my blaster fire reached up into the sky and connected with the vehicle, turning it into a ball of flame that fell from the sky and impacted the one below it sending both down into the water. Yeah, that was meant to happen that way so I don't want to hear about a lucky shot.

"Damn kid, fine shooting for your first try," Moe roared with laughter as the boat slowed down and finally stopped it's fast pace to slowly drift in the dark night.

"Yeah, thanks. Now what, Moe?" I asked looking over my shoulder at the captain of our small boat.

"Now we take a slow sail to the island and hope that we don't meet any more of those things." And with that, I felt the boat start up again as we headed toward our destination.

We had been on the water at the same slow pace for hours, each of us scanning the skies for the fliers that were hunting us. Even with the naps that Rose and I had taken during the day, I fought to keep my eyes open with the gentle rocking of the boat and the sounds of the waves lapping at its sides.

The boat once more coming to a dead stop brought me fully awake and I turned in my seat to see what the problem was. Moe was waving for me to come forward and in the quiet of the dark night, I could hear him whispering to Gus and Rose.

"What's going on?" I whispered trying to penetrate the dark ocean before us as I came up to the three standing in the wheelhouse.

"This is where you and your cousin get off my boat, kid," Moe said.

I looked at Moe and then out at the water lapping at the side of the boat. As we talked, I noticed that we were once again alongside an island, but this one being no more than one of the small bare rocks that dotted this part of the water.

"Uhm Moe, I can't swim and I don't want to be left on that small pile of rocks either."

Moe and Gus gave a tiny chuckle into the dark. "No, you and your cousin here are going to take our skiff and head to the mainland a couple of miles to the south."

"And what are you two going to do?"

"Tell them, Cassie, that they need to come with us," Rose said before Moe could answer my question. "Tell them their idea is crazy, that we will all make it."

"Okay, Moe what's up and why are we taking a small boat anywhere without you two?"

Moe pulled me gently over to the gunner position that my cousin had been in earlier and pointed at the com screen. "See all those little blips there," he said as he ran his fingers over the screen that showed over two dozen small markers.

"Yeah, so what are those?" I said having a sneaking suspicion what they were.

"They're fliers and we won't get past them without a little diversion."

"And you two and this boat will be the diversion, is what you are telling me Moe?"

"You got it in one, kid," Moe said with another of his quiet laughs.

"This really sucks Moe; you do know that, don't you?"

"Yeah, well you and your cousin need to find that ship and get you, the star map, and your parents off this planet."

"And what about you two?" I said looking over at Gus and then back at Moe.

"Listen, kid, there is no way that the aliens have brought down these fliers to this planet if they hadn't already gotten rid of most of the people on it. The ships you're looking for only hold a few people so that not all of us can get away from here anyway."

"But I thought there were two scout ships so there should be plenty of room for all of us."

"No kid sorry, but you are wrong. I saw some of the original notes from after the crash, and only one of the scout ships was in good enough condition to fly."

"Then why didn't they use it to get some help?"

Moe smiled once again at me. "They weren't sure if the aliens had followed them or if the aliens had put out trackers that could follow them back to the home world so they wanted to wait awhile to see what happened. Then the fight with the Tekis happened, then trying to make a living on this rock, people just forgot all about the ship after a time except for a few of us."

"Listen, I think Rose is right. There must be anot. . ."

"Enough talking you two, come with me," Moe said as he moved down toward the rear of the boat.

The four of us went to the back of the boat where Moe and Gus opened a hatch and muscled out a small boat and slipped it into the water. Turning to us and not waiting for any more argument, Moe lifted both of us by the back of our shirts and loaded us into the boat. That little trick of his, I thought, was getting really tiring.

After the boat stopped rocking from our abrupt disposal into the skiff, Moe bent down to explain the finer points of the vessel we were in. "Alright, girlys, this boat has a steering wheel just like a ground car so it is easy to drive. In the box there on your right is food and water, with weapons in the left box, got it?"

"Yeah, Moe we got it, but. . ." I said as I looked up at Moe and watched Gus disappear to the front of the boat.

"No listen, kid, when you get to the Teki mainland you come across any natives you ask for Suba. Got that?"

"Yeah, we got it Moe, but. . ." I started to say thinking if only I could get these two guys to listen to reason, but we all stopped moving and cocked our ears to listen to the sound of the alien ships as they passed over our rock, heading back toward where we had once been before.

"See there they go now, we can all get out of here Moe," Rose said looking up at him from the small boat.

Our two packs thumped into the bottom of the boat next

to us as Gus came back from where he had gone. "I counted three, Captain," Gus said looking at where the fliers that passed over had gone. "And I looked at the screen and saw about eight more fliers ready to join the party. If we're going, it should probably be now before any more decide to come have fun, don't you think?" Gus said in his gruff voice.

"You're right, Gus, you take the back gun and I'll take the front, and make every shot count," Moe said clapping his crewmember on his back.

"Don't I always, Captain?" Gus said with a smile that I had never seen on his face before, and then he walked over to the rear gun emplacement and begin to buckle himself into the seat.

Moe looked over at Gus for a few moments then back to us. "Alright, girlys, you go around that island across from us and then point the boat due south and head out. Run the boat at fifty percent till you hit land which should take about an hour or so. Once you hit shore, follow the shoreline around the island until you hit the starting point of the map and then head inland."

We all sat there until Moe reached over with his foot and pushed against our boat to shove us away. "Good luck girlys and find your parents, Cassie," Moe said as he headed back toward the front of the boat.

I sat down in the seat and hit the starter switch as I watched Moe and Gus head out from the rock that we had been tied to until they were lost to the dark night. Slowly we came up on the island that Moe had told us about and bit by bit we moved around it until we were lined up with the compass heading that would take us to the Teki's land.

Sitting in the smaller boat, we could feel the waves bounce us around a little as they broke against the rock we were hiding behind, but it still felt wrong to take off and leave Moe and Gus behind.

"What should we do, Cassie?" Rose asked from the dark from behind me.

I looked down at the compass that basked in the tiny red light and then glanced over my shoulder at my cousin. "Not much we can do, Rose, except follow what Moe told us to do, I guess," I said as I pushed the throttle forward to move us out from behind the island and take us to our destination.

Meeting the Tekis

Concussions and bright lights flowing up from the water and down from the sky drew our attention as we moved across the ocean. We could see that Moe and Gus were getting the better of the aliens as balls of flames that were once alien ships lit up the night air and fell into the ocean's depths.

"Maybe they will make it out in one piece," Rose said as we watched the streaks of energy coming from the sky taper off and then all but disappear.

"Yeah, maybe you're right, Rose," I said as I looked over at the quiet night sky with hope. Then it suddenly died as something large flew over our small boat causing us to rock in its turbulence.

"WHAT WAS THAT?" Rose yelled grabbing my arms and ducking into the bottom of the boat, yeah, like that would do us any good, I thought. I looked up into the sky and saw a massive shape move above us, headed to the last place that we had seen blaster fire come from.

"Rose, let go of me. We have to get out of here," I said as I disentangled myself from my cousin and sat up, pushing the throttle forward to the stops. The boat jumped forward in the water creating a small wake behind us, but all I was interested in was putting as much distance between us and whatever was up in the dark night sky.

I glanced down at the compass to make sure that we were still heading south when I heard Rose whisper, "Cassie look," and saw her point where multiple flashes were darting up into the sky.

Whatever Moe and Gus were shooting at was low to the water and moving fast toward them. The ship or whatever it was blocked out the lighter clouds in the night and I soon saw it hover above the boat that Moe and Gus were on. They were still firing all their weapons up from the boat when I was blinded by several large green flashes that appeared from the bottom of the alien ship and the large fireball that lit up the night when the boat was hit by one of those energy flashes.

I slowed the boat down and then started to turn it toward where Moe and Gus were.

"What are you doing, Cassie?" Rose asked, looking at the changing course I had us headed on.

"I can't leave them like that, Rose."

"Good, let's go get . . ." Rose started to say but was stopped as we watched a large fireball engulf the boat and ship. When the blast cleared and we could once more see in the dark, there was no boat or ship anywhere around, and then we were hit with the sound of the explosion and the concussion from it.

I stopped and watched the spot where the alien ship and Moe's boat had been and the only sound on the water was my cousin's small sob sounding behind me. After the waves from the concussion stopped lapping at our boat, I turned us around once more south and quietly headed toward the Teki Reservation.

As we moved through the water, the night sky opened up and the rain poured down on us making an already dismal night even worse than before. For most of our journey, Rose was quiet and in no mood for talking or discussing what we were going to do.

I was lost in my own thoughts, thinking over all that had happened tonight and trying to keep us headed due south as much as possible in the dark that surrounded us when Rose grabbed my arm. "Cassie listen, what is that?"

I stopped the boat and listened to the sound as the rain finally died down to a slow drizzle. It sounded like a low boom with a wash of rushing water. "I don't know, Rose, but keep your eyes open," I said as I moved the power to the boat up and we slowly cut through the water toward whatever the sound was.

As we moved through the water, I noticed that we seemed to be moving faster as the sound became louder. I stared at the dark night willing my eyes to pierce the blackness to see what was up ahead of us when a flash of lighting lit up the sky and we saw what was making the noise.

In front of us were two large cliffs, one on the right and one on the left, extending as far to either side as I could see in that brief flash of light, with an opening between them. The booming sound was the water hitting the rocks at the bottom of the cliff and the rushing sound was made by the water crashing through the opening.

"Head between the cliffs, Cassie," Rose said with fear in her voice.

I glanced back at my cousin and then back at the rocks as another flash of lightening lit up the night. Really no kidding, I thought, as I steered the boat toward the middle of the opening before us.

Rose wrapped her arms around me with a shout as I felt the boat get lifted by a wave and we stormed past the cliffs on each side of us. Then another flash of lightning lit up the night and I saw the canyon we had entered narrowed down and that we were headed toward what looked like a solid rock wall in front of us.

I threw the power of the small boat to full and turned the steering wheel over to turn us away from the rock wall when I saw that the water was curving around one side of the cliff. Just before we hit the wall we shot forward over a small falls and then into a large lake.

The momentum of the water and full power from the little boat bounced us about a third of the way across the lake like a skipping stone before I slowed us down. After that we were finally drifting on the quiet water of the lake, heck even the rain and lightning had stopped for once.

I looked at the water around us and the beach and woods that were in front of us and thought that it might be a good idea to wait until daylight, what there is of it, to do any exploring.

"Now what, Cassie?" Rose asked a death grip still on my arms.

"Now I think, cousin," I said as I slowly detached her hands from my arms. "I think we rest and then look where we have ended up in a better light."

"Yeah, but where do we rest? I don't want to be near those woods at night, at least not until we know where we are."

"No problem," I said as I steered toward a small rock jutting out of the water. As we got closer I could see some small trees growing on the rock. "Here, find some rope in one of those boxes so we can tie up to these trees," I said as I bumped the boat up next to the rock and grabbed hold of some of the foliage that hung over the water as Rose dove into the boxes to find some rope.

"Here we go, Cassie," Rose said as she came up with two lengths of rope in her hands.

We tied both the front and back of the boat to the trees hanging from the rock so that it hid us from the beach and gave us some overhead cover in case any fliers came snooping about.

"Now what, Cassie?" Rose said after we had finished tying the boat up.

"Now, my dear cousin, we eat some of the food that is in those boxes and we get some sleep. Then comes daylight and we see what kind of supplies we have and then we head to the land to see where we are."

With that both of us grabbed some food packs and pulled the warming strips on them. We gobbled down a quiet hot meal and then we both snuggled down together in the bottom of the boat in a couple of blankets to keep warm as slumber took both of us deep within its arms.

I woke up with a subdued light shining down through the trees and laid there wondering if all that had happened to us was a dream or maybe better one long nightmare, but the slight rocking of the boat that was our bed brought me back to reality.

"Rose? You up?" I whispered rolling over and looking at

my cousin.

"Yeah, I'm up, Cassie, even though I wish I was back asleep and this was all a dream."

"Yeah, I know, I was thinking the same thing."

Rose sat up and looked around at that part of the lake we could see from our position near the rocks. "Now what, Cassie?"

I looked at my cousin, my temper flaring a little because she thought I had all the answers to the problems we seemed to be running into lately. "Why do you keep asking me what to do? It's not like I have ever been in this situation before."

"Sorry, Cassie, just you're so, I don't know, got it all together when we get in a tight space," Rose said as she hung her head and looked down at the bottom of the boat.

Oh great, I thought, I've peeved off my best friend and who knew maybe the last of my family. I slid over next to Rose and gave her a tight squeeze. "Sorry, Rose, I guess I'm as scared as you and I wish Moe was here with us to get us out of this mess."

"Yeah, me too."

We sat around in the boat for awhile feeling sorry for ourselves when our stomachs announced that we hadn't had any breakfast yet with some low volume grumbling. The sound seemed to break up our pity party and we giggled like when we were younger as we dived into the food box to get some grub.

As we ate breakfast, I looked around the parts of the lake that we were on trying to find a way out of here. Right away I saw that we weren't going back the way we had come since the waterfall we came over was big enough that we weren't going back up it.

The whole lake, from what I could see, was surrounded by high rocky cliffs and unless we all of a sudden grew wings we weren't going up those either, so I guess that left the beach behind us.

Rose was looking around as I was and she must have come to the same conclusion as I did. "I think the only way to go is to hit the beach."

"Yeah, you're right," I said as I stood to untie the boat from the trees we had anchored to last night. The boat rocked a little and Rose gave a little squeal of fright. "Oh don't be such a scaredy cat," I said as I looked over at her. "I thought that maybe when we got to the beach we could take a quick dip in the water since it has been awhile since I had a bath."

"That sounds good, Cassie," Rose said as she threw some leftover food over the side of the boat.

We both stopped as the food hit the water and it began to bubble and boil with turbulence from all these small fish with the biggest set of teeth I had ever seen. As the water settled once again I looked over at Rose and saw that her eyes were as big around as mine probably were. "Uhm maybe we skip that bath until we get somewhere else, Rose?"

"Oh yeah, I think I smell fine, Cassie," Rose said with a small nervous twitter.

I carefully now moved to the front of the boat and started the engine and headed us around the rock and toward the beach ahead at a slow pace. "Hey Moe said there were some weapons in one of those boxes, let's see what we got in case me meet someone not as nice as Moe," I said over my shoulder, thinking of the small blasters that each of us carried at our sides.

I heard Rose rummaging in one of the boxes and then her laugh as she leaned a small blast rifle against the side of my seat. "Oh yeah, we got weapons alright, think you know how to use one of those?"

I glanced at the rifle and saw that it was a make that my parents had taught me to use and nodded. "Yeah, any baddies come around; I'll know what to do with that, Rose."

"Good, I got one too, so bring on the baddies," Rose said with a laugh. It was good to see that after all we had been through she still had her sense of humor.

The ride across the rest of the lake was pretty boring, but tense, as we both looked for any openings in the cliff walls and tried to keep any eye on our destination at the same time. By the time we got close to land, we saw the beach to be our only option out of here so I headed the boat slowly toward the center of the sandy landing spot.

I glanced back at Rose as we neared the spot I was aiming for and saw that she was crouched down in the boat, the blast rifle aiming toward the trees we were approaching. "If something comes out of the trees make sure it isn't friendly before you pull the trigger, Rose."

"And you want me to find that out how?" Rose asked with a small chuckle.

I thought about that for a second and figured that anything coming out of those trees probably wouldn't be friendly, since we knew no one here, wherever here was. "Yeah, you're right, blast anything that comes out of the trees."

'Don't worry, cousin, way ahead of you on that score."

As we neared the beach, I put full power to the small craft figuring that I wanted to drive it as far up the shore as I could, because there was no way I was stepping out into these waters. The boat scraped bottom then kept moving with the power handle full forward until the front half was up on the beach and I could hear the engine screaming trying to drive it further up onto the sand. I slammed the throttle back and cut the engine and in the sudden quiet, I grabbed the blast rifle next to me and pointed it out toward the tree line.

The two of us sat there, moving our weapons back and forth watching for some monster to jump out of the trees and charge us, but the quiet lingered until the rifle I was holding started to get heavy in my arms.

The clink on the side of the boat I heard was Rose resting her own weapon down on the side of the craft. "I don't think there is anything out there, Cassie," she whispered.

I glanced back at my cousin and then back at the trees. "Yeah, I think you're right, but let's do this the smart way. I'm going to get everything out of the boat while you keep a watch out on the tree line."

"Sure, Cassie; whatever you say."

I lowered my weapon and then crawled out of the boat, keeping my eyes peeled for that monster that I just knew was going to come out of the trees any second. I guess maybe we should have been watching the water as I heard a large splash and saw a huge double-headed serpent rise out of the water behind the boat.

I let out a yelp as I grabbed my rifle from the boat and tripped over my own two feet, falling backward onto the sand. I tried to raise my rifle to shoot whatever that thing was as I heard Rose give a scream and saw her bail out the other side of the boat.

The two heads came crashing down on the back end of the boat tearing and grinding it into small pieces. As the heads came back up once more with growls and roars of anger, I finally found the trigger with my finger and let it have a full charge of energy from my rifle. Luckily for us, Rose also found hers. As both of our weapons burst apart the beast's heads, it slipped beneath the water which was suddenly churning with those small little fish again. We each watched in horror as those little fish stripped the serpent down to the bone in mere seconds. After a little bit of the water bubbling, churning, and turning a sickly green from the creature's blood it cleared and settled down to its peaceful tranquil self once more. Yeah, this was so not the water to take a bath in.

I jumped up and ran around what used to be our boat to check on my cousin, but skidded to a dead stop when I saw her rifle barrel swing toward me. "Whoa, whoa it's me, Rose."

I saw her smile and then relax her grip on the trigger so I walked over and gave her a hand up from the ground. "Well I guess we walk from here on out," she said as we both stood looking at what was left of the boat.

"Yeah, I guess that we do," I said even though I didn't really think that was ever in doubt.

"What was that thing?" I asked looking out toward the water hoping that it was single and didn't have any family around here.

"I don't know what that was, but when I traveled with my dad I heard that there were creatures on the Teki

Reservation and in the waters around it that weren't on our island."

"Oh, great that's all we need now. First aliens, then ships, fliers, and star maps, and now we have to deal with unknown creatures, sounds like a badly written monster movie if you ask me."

"Well, it could be worse I. . ." Rose said as she turned toward the tree line and her eyes bugged out of her head.

I slowly turned and saw that we were surrounded by Tekis or at least that was who I thought they were. "You really had to go and say that, didn't you?" I whispered out the side of my mouth.

"I'm sorry, Cassie," Rose sobbed as the nearest of the Tekis motioned with their own weapons for us to drop ours. Since we were surrounded and all their weapons were pointed at us, it seemed like a pretty good idea to do what they wanted us to do.

"No worries, Rose," I said as I looked over our captors. Each of them looked like a human except that they all stood about six feet tall with green skin and red eyes, but the most unusual thing about them was that each of them had four arms. Two of their arms were set on the shoulder like we have and then they had a set of arms that were attached to their waist.

It made for a pretty weird sight, seeing the Teki for the first time, but then I had seen my first alien just the other day, so what was one more strange creature more or less.

We all stood there for several minutes, no one making a move or making a sound when my cousin stepped forward toward the group in front of us. "Uhm hi, can you help us?"

The Teki in front of us stood there, their eyes never wavering from us or for that matter their weapons either. I looked more closely at their weapons, trying to figure a way out of our situation but didn't hold out much hope as I saw that most of the warriors before us had crossbows and long spears, besides the various knives each carried at their sides.

"Okay guys," I said as I stepped up next to my cousin. "You can either help us, let us go, or kill us, but let's pick one and get going before I die of boredom."

"Yeah, right," Rose said. "You can kill us, but you can't eat us, right?"

"Uhm Rose, not helping," I said looking over at the Teki once more trying to remember just what they did eat.

One of the Teki stepped forward and gave us a fierce once over then turned toward the rest of the group and started to laugh in a loud rough voice when all the others joined him in his merriment.

Rose and I stood there watching as the group before us broke up in laughter and all the weapons were lowered toward the ground. I looked over at my cousin and she shrugged her shoulders as she seemed as puzzled as I was.

After a few seconds of this behavior, it stopped as fast as it started. "We not eat you, you too small and scrawny, no meat," the Teki who had started the laughter said as he moved over and stood before us.

"Hey, I'm not scrawny!" I said with as much indignation as I could put in my voice. "I'm just short."

Rose looked over at me and lightly tapped me on the arm. "Uhm Cassie, now look who's not helping."

"Oh yeah, sorry," I said feeling my face go red, but what can I say I really have a problem with my height.

"Who you?" the Teki that stood before us asked.

"I'm Cassie and this is my cousin Rose, uhm who are you?"

"Suba, leader of Teki," the Teki said as he first pointed to himself then back at the group around us.

"Then you're the person Moe told us to find so we must be on the Teki Reservation," Rose blurted out before I smacked her on her arm. She looked over at me and once more shrugged her shoulders. "Sorry Cassie."

It was quiet for a few seconds once again as I saw Suba think over what Rose had inadvertently told him. "You friends with Moe?"

"Yes we are, and he told us to look for you after we got here," I whispered hoping like hell that Moe knew what he was talking about when he sent us here.

"And Cassie's parents were here also, you know looking for a ship," Rose said.

That seemed to get a response from the group around us as the Teki mumbled to each other in their language and Suba gave us another one of his searching looks. "What kind of ship you parents look for?" he asked.

I looked at Suba and the rest of the people around us and figured what the hell they were either on our side or they were on the alien's side, but now was not the time to mince words. "The ship we are looking for is the first ship that the humans used to come down from the sky," I said pointing up into the air and making the motion as if to show a ship landing on the ground.

"Oh, you mean starship?" Suba said with a large grin shaping his face.

"Yeah, right a starship, so you know what we are looking for?" I asked.

Suba nodded his head and glanced back at the group around us and then back at us. "Yes I know starship, you come with us."

"And if we don't come with you?" I asked.

"Then you get eaten by Zeeky," Suba said as he shrugged his shoulders and stood there looking at us. "And then we come back tomorrow and take what they leave."

I didn't know what a Zeeky was, but from the looks on all

the Teki around us, I figured it wasn't good. "Yeah, I think going with you might be better."

"Yes better for Zeeky too as no meat on you two," Suba said with a grin as he turned with the rest of the Tekis and headed toward the woods.

A Long March

"Hey wait a second," I said to the retreating backs of the people in front of us. They all, as one, stopped and turned and looked at me as Suba stepped back toward us. "We need to get our things together."

"How long you take?" Suba asked with some exasperation filling his voice.

Guys must have a hot date, I thought, as all of the Teki around us danced from one foot to another, anxious to get wherever they were going. "Uhm, a few minutes Suba."

Suba looked at us for a few seconds and then glanced up at the sky. Finally, he barked an order and two unhappy looking Teki walked over to us and stood on either side of what was left of our boat. "These two show you way." With that, all the Teki, except the two that stood by us, disappeared into the tree line

Rose and I looked over at each other and then at the two guides that stood looking at everything but us. "Well I guess we should get our things together and follow them, don't you think?" I asked my cousin.

"Yeah, sure, Cassie," Rose said as we both moved over to the boat to see what we could salvage.

It took us more than a few minutes to look through the wreckage, but we were lucky that we found our backpacks, along with some food that hadn't been damaged too badly, but the best find I thought was that we also came up with extra energy packs for the rifles and blasters we had.

Suba and the Teki seemed pretty friendly for now, but there were still aliens and other unknown creatures out there and I wasn't quite ready yet to put all my trust or life in the hands of the Teki.

We gathered everything we could and stuffed our packs until they were ready to burst. Throwing them on our backs we were finally ready to move out. "Okay, guys we're ready," I said to the two Teki that Suba had left behind for guides.

All through our packing and scavenging, the two Tekis had been jittery and bouncy while they muttered between the two of them. Now that we were ready to go, they stood there watching us with those strange red eyes of theirs.

"Uhm, we're ready guys. Lead on," I said pointing in the

direction that the others had gone before us. Both men stood there looking at us. Okay, this was getting annoying. "Well I'm going," I said as I headed toward the path I'd seen the others take.

"Yeah, me too," Rose said as she ran to catch up to me.

As we hit the path, I heard laughter close behind us and saw that the two Tekis had moved up with us and they soon passed us to lead us up the trail with those long legs of theirs. "Great sense of humor these guys got hmm, Rose?"

"Oh yeah, really funny guys here," she said hiking the pack on her back and settling it better on her shoulders. "A real laugh a minute these guys are, Cassie."

We moved at the fast clip that our guides set. In some spots, it felt almost like I had to run to keep up with those in front of us. After what seemed like hours, I was so out of breath and I could see that even Rose was breathing harder than usual.

"Okay, that's it," I said as I threw my pack down on the ground and sat down with it. "I need a rest."

"Yeah, me too," Rose said as she copied my actions.

The two Teki stood there looking out at the trees around us and shook their heads at our rebellion. One of the Teki then came over to us and pointed up the trail after a few seconds and started to say something in his language. After about two minutes of this, I looked up at him and shrugged my shoulders and said, "We rest here."

Both of them stood there looking around the trees once again and this time, I saw that they weren't so much annoyed at us as they seemed to be afraid of something. I concentrated on the nearest Teki, wondering if I could pick up what they were afraid of as I could with humans.

I didn't get a clear image of whatever it was that was frightening them, more like a shadow of something long with a tail and elongated claws and teeth. I tried to get more, but a fierce animal scream off in the trees broke my concentration.

"Zeeky," whispered the two men and then they turned and started down the trail not even looking back to see if we would follow.

I looked over at Rose and saw her eyes go wide as she scrambled up off the ground. I was right behind her as another scream echoed once more through the trees.

"Zeeky?" I said as we both shouldered our packs and headed out behind the Teki guides.

"Yeah, maybe we rest later, you think?" Rose said now breathing harder as we ran to catch up with the guides.

"Yeah, you're right, cousin, we rest later," I said looking back and forth expecting any second to be attacked by whatever was out there in the trees.

"Hey, guys wait up. We're coming," Rose yelled at the Teki.

They must have understood our intent because they stopped and waited as we caught up to them, and then passed them as another scream came once more from the trees behind us.

We kept moving at this fast pace for quite awhile with one of the Teki men in front of us and one behind until the trail started to climb out of the trees. As we climbed higher into scrub trees and then brush, I noticed that our guides slowed their pace and seemed to relax some.

The top of the trail hit a ridgeline that gave us a wonderful view of the land around us. Rose and I stopped and looked back down at the way we came. I could see the lake below us looking like a small puddle of water in the middle of a valley surrounded by high walls of rock. The path we had taken to reach this point wound through the trees sometimes lost beneath them, sometimes showing up on the side of the hill we had trudged up like a brown scar across its side. Turning around we looked out from our high spot and saw that we indeed had landed on the main Teki land.

Both of the Teki walked back to us and then sat down on the ground. "Rest now," one of the men said as he pointed at us and then at the ground.

Both Rose and I threw our packs down on the ground and then laid the rifles we had been carrying across them. "Guess we must be in a safe zone, Cassie."

"Yeah, I guess so," I said looking along the trail that led

along the ridge we were on. I pulled the map that we had found in my parent's work room out of my pocket and spread it on my lap as Rose scooted closer to me.

"So how close are we, Cassie?"

I looked around the land below us seeing the trees and what looked like clearings and buildings further out along a coastline to the right of us. Then I followed the coast until my eyes came to a small mountain range across from where we now sat.

"I think that that is where we want to go, Rose," I said pointing to one mountain higher than the rest of the range I was looking at.

"You think these guys will help us get there, and if they do is the ship still there?"

"I don't know, Rose, we have to take it one thing at a time. Moe seemed to trust Suba, and we trusted Moe so let's figure it will all work out for the best."

"Okay Cassie, I trusted Moe too so like you said one thing at a time."

I folded the map and slipped it into my pocket as the two Teki once more stood up and pointed down the trail on the ridgeline. "Zeeky home," the tallest said as he pointed back at the valley we had left. "Our home," he then pointed to the land below us and then both of them started to walk down the trail without looking back to see if we were following.

"I guess rest break is over and we are going to their home," I said as I stood, picked up the rifle and shouldered my pack.

"Yeah, we follow them to their home and hope for the best, guess it can't be any worse than the Zeeky home," Rose said as we followed the two Teki already ahead of us and moving once more at a fast clip.

We moved along the ridgeline to the right toward the ocean and the cultivated areas below us. The smell of salt air from the water grew heavier the closer we got and before we hit the end of the ridge we turned down a path to lead us away from the valley behind us.

When we hit the bottom of the trail, the Teki once more took a short break and Rose and I pulled out some meal packs to grab some food. I hadn't realized just how hungry I was until I pulled the heating strip and the aroma of the heated meal drifted up through the air around us. My stomach gave a little growl of satisfaction at the smell that came from the meal package.

The Teki watched us for a few minutes as we gobbled down our food and then muttered between themselves with some chuckles thrown in for good measure. Feeling pretty full, I walked over to them and offered what was left in the pack I had, which when I burped, had a sort of fishy taste to it.

The two of them passed the package back and forth between them, smelling its contents with some more muttering and chuckling then handed it back to me with wrinkled noses and shaking heads. "Well okay then more for me, I guess," I said as I watched them reach down into the pouches they carried at their sides and pulled out some dried, pungent smelling concoction and stuffed it into their mouths.

All I could think as I walked back to Rose was that these guy's sense of smell and taste was way off if they would eat something that smelled that bad over one of the meal packs we had, not that the meal packs were ever considered a delicacy where we came from either, but it was a lot better than what they were chewing down on.

"Hey Cassie I'm thirsty, how's the water in your canteen?" Rose said sloshing around the little bit she had in the bottom of hers.

"Yeah, I need some water too," I said turning to our guides and shaking my empty canteen in the air. "Water?"

Both of them looked at us with a blank stare for a second then one of them smiled and hopped up from where he was sitting and grabbed our two canteens and disappeared into the trees beside us.

The other Teki settled back and started once more eating his meal until we heard a scream, which I thought we had left back in the valley behind us. The sound came from the direction the Teki had taken a few minutes ago to get our water. All three of us hopped up and ran toward the noise as another scream sounded and then silence. We three burst out into a clearing as I saw a dark shadow dragging the Teki into the bushes across from us.

Both Rose and I had our rifles to our shoulders and let go a couple of shots each before the dark shadow and the Teki disappeared into the gathering night that had now started to fall upon us. The Teki with us walked over to a small stream that flowed through the clearing and picked up our canteens and handed them over to us. "We go now," he said in a whisper, looking back over his shoulder at where the shadow and his companion had disappeared just seconds ago.

"What was that?" Rose asked as she took her canteen and stuck it on the side of her pack after taking a quick slug of water from it.

"Zeeky."

I walked over to the stream, keeping a careful eye on the bushes across from us and looked down at the ground for any tracks. What a saw was a set of paw prints that were almost as big around as my head. Each print looked like someone had set a large round disk down in the mud and then put four other smaller disks around one side. Whatever it was, it was very big and very fast and I didn't think I wanted to meet something that took out a Teki that quickly and quietly.

"But I thought you said the Zeeky's home was over there?" Rose said as she pointed up toward the ridgeline and the valley beyond it.

"Yes, Zeeky home," the Teki said as he pointed in the same direction that Rose had. "Zeeky hunt," he then said sweeping both his arms around to take in the land we were in.

"We go now," he then said as he turned toward the trail we had left.

"But what about. . ." Rose started to say and then stopped as the Teki came back and stood before us.

Our Teki guide shrugged his shoulders and then pointed toward the way we had been headed. "We go now," he said once more and then turned and disappeared into the trees toward the path.

"Yeah, but Cassie, we can't leave him here, can we?" Rose asked looking once more into the bushes that the Zeeky and his prey had disappeared into.

"Let's go, Rose," I said as I grabbed her by the arm and headed after our guide. "Even if we did find him, I doubt that there would be much left to worry about."

"Oh yeah, right didn't think that through, did I?" Rose said as we found the trail once more and caught sight of our guide.

"No worries Rose," I told her as we both glanced over at where we had been and then hurried up once more to catch up with the Teki in front of us.

Once more we walked through the trees as the dark descended on us. I noticed that Rose and I kept moving closer to our guide until we were almost tripping over his heels. Surprising what a little motivation like becoming some creature's dinner will do for your speed and stamina in a long walk.

We popped out of the trees into open fields where some grain was waving in the night air like the waves on the ocean. Our guide stopped for a few seconds and then looked down the trail we were on pointing toward some distant lights. "Home," he said and then started walking down the trail once more.

Finding the Ship

Now that we were out of the trees and hopefully out of the Zeeky's hunting range, I could feel the day's adventures start to catch up with me. I fought to keep my eyes open as my feet plodded along the dirt path we were traveling. A small cry behind me shook me out of my stupor and I looked to the rear to see Rose sitting on the ground in a heap.

I looked back at our Teki guide and saw that he was standing there exchanging glances between my cousin and I and where his home lights shone in the dark. We must have won out because he soon moved past me and walked over to where Rose was and squatted down next to her. "You rest till day," he said, his restless eyes roving the waving grain around us.

I plopped down where I stood about five feet from them with a loud sigh. "Yeah, I think I'll plant myself here if you don't mind," and with that I leaned back on my pack, closed my eyes and let sleep take me away from this nightmare.

I don't know if it was the strange voices that woke me or the uncomfortable ground that I was lying on, but wake up I did way too soon as my body and mind complained to me that what I needed was more sleep. I rolled over and sat up and saw that someone had moved Rose next to me and that she was as about as awake as I was.

"Hey Cassie, guess it's time to get up?" she whispered as she looked over at the group of Teki that was gathered around our guide.

"Yeah, I guess so, how about we go see what is up with these guys?" I said as I stood up, feeling every ache and creak from my body. I stretched out, watching Rose move slowly up from the ground like some old women and didn't feel so bad about being so stoved up from our travels and sleeping on the ground last night.

We walked over to the silent group that just moments ago were interrogating our guide with gusto. "Well, are we going on now or waiting here?" I asked as we both settled down in front of the group before us.

"I go to home now," our guide said as the others started off for tree line behind us.

"So where are they going?" Rose asked as the group of

Teki walked past us.

"Hunt Zeeky," our guide said and without looking back at us or the others he headed off toward the village that we could see in the distance by the light of day.

Rose and I threw our packs over our shoulders and fell in behind our guide, following him when my stomach let out a growl to let me know that I hadn't eaten any breakfast yet. "Here let me dig out a meal pack for you," Rose said as she slowed down to get behind me and get to my pack.

I could feel her tug and dig around in my pack and then pull something out of it as I heard a growl of hunger from her stomach. Never stopping her stride, Rose stepped up next to me and handed me one of the meal packs that she had found.

"Here cousin," she said as ripped the heating strip off of the second pack. "I owe you a meal pack since I grabbed one from you, Cassie."

"Yeah, like I'm really worried about it, share and share alike I always say, cousin," I said opening my own heating strip and my stomach really growling now as the smell of the food from the meal packs permeated the air.

I was going to offer our guide some of our food once more when I noticed that he was again eating that leather looking meat from his own pouch, so I dug into my own food as we walked onward.

By the time we were done with our meal, I could see that

we had come quite a ways down the road and that we weren't that far from the Teki's home. As we got closer, I could see a mud wall that was about eight to ten feet high that had sharp stakes embedded into it pointing outward. I guess those were to keep anything from going over the wall and into the village, I thought looking at the stakes and wondering what could get up a wall that high.

Another hour or so brought us right to the front gate that I could see was made out of thick, sturdy pieces of wood banded together to form an impenetrable-looking barrier. What really bothered me was that that barrier was still closed.

Our guide was about ten feet in front of us and as we neared the walls a small door opened in the gate and he disappeared into it and then it closed. Both Rose and I rushed over to the door and stood there, our mouths hanging open in disbelief that the Teki would bring us this far just to leave us sitting here outside their village.

"Now what do we do, Cassie?"

"I don't know, I just don't know."

From our left, someone cleared their throat and then spoke. "Uhm, maybe I can help you two ladies?"

Rose stood there as though she hadn't heard the voice as I

turned to look at who had spoken. I saw I tall, thin human leaning against the wall looking the two of us over with interest. "And who are you?" I asked.

"Who is who?" asked Rose searching the area I was looking at.

Oh damn, this was a ghost, I thought, as I saw a small smile spread across the man's face. I turned back to Rose and pointed at where he stood; still leaning against the wall as though he had all the time in the world. Well, I guess he probably did since he was dead and didn't have much to do.

"It's a ghost again, Rose."

"Like the one down in your work room?"

"I don't know. Guess we will find out."

I turned back to the man who was now looking at our exchange with some amusement. "I take it she can't see or hear me, but you can?"

"Yeah, you're right. Who are you anyways?" I asked.

"I? Well, my name is Jack. Gunners mate first class Jack C. Burke to be precise."

"Well hello Jack C. Burke. My name is Cassie and this is my cousin Rose, nice to meet you."

"Nice to meet you too, Cassie. You look just like the commander, are you related?"

"Yeah, I guess so or at least that is what I was told, Jack C. Burke."

"It's just Jack, now like I said before how can I help you, young ladies?"

"Well the Teki bought us here and we thought that maybe they would help us find the original ship's crash site."

"And you want to find this why?" Jack said, giving us a searching look.

"We need to find it to get to one of the scout ships, rescue my parents and then get away from the aliens that were chasing the ship before it crashed here, that's why Jack."

"Oh, the aliens are here?" Jack said bounding off the wall and looking around as though the aliens would appear in front of us at any moment.

"Yeah, they are, so if you can help us now is the time to say so, Jack," I said as Rose and I stood there hoping that a ghost could get us out of our particular predicament.

After a few moments, Jack smiled and then looked at the wall before us. "Okay, I have a plan I think, but first, I need to ask you a question. Am I the only ghost that you can see?"

"Uhm no, in fact back home we had a ghost named Jolly that I could see and talk to."

"Jolly, you mean the Jolly from the ship; a big loudmouthed

blowhard that thought a lot of himself?"

"Yeah, that is Jolly alright I guess, even though he was a friend of mine, Jack."

"Okay, no offense meant, Cassie, just needed to make sure that I wasn't the only one you could see."

"Alright, so what is your plan, Jack?"

"Oh right – my plan, well my plan is, is that you and the other young lady here take this path along the side of the village and follow it along the trail, and the crew that died along the way from the crash site will guide you to the ship."

"Uhm okay, I guess that could work even though we do have a map," I said pulling out the map that we had taken from my parent's work room.

"Well yes that will help, but even with a map, after all this time, things change and it would still take you time to find the ship. With our help, I think we can lead you right to where the ship is resting."

"What is he saying, Cassie?" Rose said, impatiently hopping from one foot to the other staring at the spot on the wall that I was talking to.

I glanced at my cousin glad that she didn't think I was a total loony and looked back at Jack. "Okay, I guess we go with your idea since we have no choice, really."

"Yes, I think you had better," Jack said looking at the sky over my shoulder. "And I think you had better move along right now."

I threw a glance once more behind me and saw what Jack was looking at just as the sound of the alien ship reached our ears. "Now what, Cassie," Rose whispered in fright.

"We listen to the ghost and run this way," I said as I grabbed my cousin's arm and pulled her along the path that paralleled the wall. We ran, following Jack along the wall until we came to the end of the path which led around to another trail and another set of closed village gates.

We stopped for a second to catch a breath and to get our bearings. I could see that on this side of the wall, the trees ran almost down to the village and that if we made them we could probably lose ourselves within them.

"Okay now what, Jack?" I said between gulps of air.

"Now you find the ship."

"Yeah, but when we find the ship, how are we to figure out how to fly it?"

"Oh, that's easy. Emma will help you there."

"Uhm, who's Emma? Another ghost?"

"No more time to talk ladies, go. Because this is as far as I can go, but you will come upon many of my crewmembers and passengers like her, and they will lead you on to the ship," he said as he pointed down the trail to another specter standing at the edge of the woods just before he disappeared. About ten feet away from us, a small woman was waving us on as I looked over at Rose to see if she was ready to move yet. "We need to move, can you run?"

Rose looked at me sideways and smiled before she took off at a trot. "Just try and keep up, shorty," she threw over her shoulder as she passed the ghost still waving at me from the edge of the tree line.

I caught up with Rose as the female ghost disappeared and I saw another one appear on a trail leading to the right and up toward the mountains before us. "This way Rose," I said as I veered toward our next guide getting some satisfaction that my smart-alecky cousin who now had to keep up with my pace instead of her long-legged gait since she couldn't see the ghosts.

We moved up the trail following the dead who hadn't survived the injuries from the ship's crash or the long march down off of the mountain. As we passed them, I could see men, women, and even children lining the path, some singularly, and others in small groups all waving us on toward the ship's last resting place.

Numerous times flights of alien ships flew overhead, but we were so deep within the heavy trees that I thought that they had no chance of spotting us. It was the aliens on the ground that concerned me as we could hear them blunder around below us in the heavy tangle of terrain when we stopped for a short breather.

"Why do you think the Teki gave us up, Cassie?" Rose asked, leaning against a tree on one of our breaks.

"I think the aliens gave them a choice – either them or us. Really can't blame them, guess humans would have done the same thing."

"Yeah, I guess you are right, but you think the Teki are going to help them find us in this stuff?"

"If they were I think we would be staring at the aliens right now instead of listening to them fumble around down below us."

"Yeah, guess so," Rose said as she pushed off of her tree and looked around at the trail and foliage. "Which way, Cassie?"

I looked up the trail we had been following all day and saw a small boy who was standing off to the side pointing up at a little stream that gurgled down the hillside. "This way," I said heading over and following our new guide's directions.

We each took a quick drink from the stream and then started the climb through the trees once more. As we climbed, I noticed that the angle of the hill was getting steeper and that Rose and I had to use the trees around us and each other to get up the hill.

As the last of my strength was waning and night was once again falling, we broke out onto a flat area on the mountain side. "Oh, I need to rest for a second, Cassie," Rose said plopping down on the ground and leaning back on a thick tree for a backrest.

I sat down and saw the valley below spread out in all its glory. I didn't really appreciate just how high we had climbed today until I saw the tiny twinkling lights of the Teki village far below us.

Then looking up, I observed that we were just below the top of the mountain and that come morning we were going to run into some problems. For above this area that we were resting on, the tree line thinned out to rock and small scrubs and any alien ship passing overhead wouldn't miss us.

Rose looked over at me and followed my line of sight and then grimaced as she stood up. "Maybe if we wait until dark, we can make it up there without being spotted."

"Yeah, maybe, but I wonder how high this ship is and where it is exactly?"

"How about the map, Cassie," Rose said as she walked over to where I sat and slid down next to me.

"Oh yeah, forgot about that. Just so used to following the ghosts up here," I said as I pulled the paper map out of my pocket and spread it out on my lap.

We both looked down at the map and studied the area

around us with the few minutes of light that was left us. I was pulling out my canteen from my pack for a quick sip of water when a voice near my shoulder startled me. "Why are you girls sitting here? Shouldn't you be getting to my ship before you have aliens all over this area?"

"Oh damn," I said as I jumped up from where I had been sitting throwing the map and my canteen in two different directions.

"What is it, Cassie?" Rose said as she rolled away from me and came up to her knees with her blaster held at the ready. Her eyes were wide and she scanned the area looking for the cause of my fright.

I looked over at the man that was standing before me and could tell right away that this was another ghost from the wreck of the ship. "Uhm so not funny," I said as I looked at the man that resembled my momma and aunt in his eyes and certain facial features like the nose and mouth.

"Sorry been so long since we had anyone up here, I couldn't resist," the man said with a grin and small laugh. Yeah, I definitely knew that grin and laugh so well from my momma and her sister, Rose's momma.

"Another ghost, Cassie?" Rose said as she put her blaster away.

I glanced over at my cousin and then back at the man in front of me. "Oh yeah, but I think that this one is a relative of ours," I said as I went over and picked up my canteen and the map I had dropped in my fright.

"Ahh, so you two must be some great, great, something or other grandkids of mine?"

"Yes, I think we are if you were the Captain of the ship and Cassie was your wife."

The grin melted and a wistful look crossed his face. "Yes, I was the Captain and Cassie was my wife and my best friend in all of space."

"Well, Captain you will be proud to know that Cassie got most of your people down off this mountain and they set up a new settlement."

"Well that's good to know and now the aliens are back, right?"

"Yeah, they are and we need to find this scout ship and save my parents from the aliens. Think you can help us with that, Captain?"

The smile returned and the Captain glanced back over his shoulder and then back at me. "Why of course, Cassie, you're only about a mile or so from the main ship."

"We are?"

"We are what?" asked Rose looking at me with curiosity burning in her eyes.

I looked at Rose and then back at the tree line before us. "The Captain here says we are only about a mile or so from the ship, Rose."

"Oh thank God, so let's go find it, Cassie."

"Yeah, right, Rose," I said as I looked over once more at the Captain. "Well sir, if you could take us there, please."

"Why sure, anything for my descendants," the Captain said with a chuckle and headed off toward the trees ahead of us.

We followed the Captain through the trees in the dark night that had finally fallen on us like a thick heavy winter blanket. "Uhm just one question, Captain," I asked as we wove through the trees around us for a while.

"Sure Cassie, what is it?"

"Well, if we are close to the ship why haven't the aliens found it by now? 'Cause I know that they have had fliers over this area looking for us."

"Well, when we came down on the side of this mountain, it wasn't my finest of landings and between the ship breaking up and time there isn't much left of the old girl."

"Oh so do you think that this scout ship will be in any condition to fly?"

"Yes I think so, but only Emma will know for sure," the Captain said as he stopped before a dark wall that popped out of the night before us."

"Who is this Emma?" I asked as I stopped next to Rose and the Captain and looked up at the wall before us and then realized that it wasn't a wall at all, but part of some large craft lying in the woods.

"Oh," both Rose and I whispered as we stepped forward and touched the cold metal.

"Wow, this is so cool, Cassie," Rose said in a whisper.

"Yeah, it is," I whispered back in awe as I stood back and looked up at the size of what I could see in the dark. "But how do we get in."

"Follow me, young ladies," the Captain said as he headed along the right side of the ship. In the dark night, I could make out parts, large and small. The pieces spread out around the main part of the ship we were walking by.

Rose noticed the debris field around the ship also as I heard a low whistle and whisper from behind me. "Wow, they really tore up the ship when it came down."

The Captain stopped and looked over at Rose with a frown. "Let's see you do better, young lady."

I smiled at her and then looked back over at the Captain. "Sorry sir she can't hear you, I guess I was the only one in the family that has this little quirk."

"Oh, well that's okay, but anyways here is how you get in

my ship," the Captain said pointing to a large hole in the side of the metal.

"Uhm thanks, Captain, but where do we go once we are in there?" I asked as I sized up once more the dimensions of the ship before us.

"Oh, that's easy, once you are in there follow the passageway back the way we came and you will find a small hanger bay where the ship is waiting for you. When you get to the ship, you will see an airlock on the left side of the hull with a keypad next to the door. Punch in the code 4553 and you will open the airlock and then Emma will take it from there."

"I take it you aren't coming with us then?"

"No, I think you young ladies will be fine from here on out on your own, so good luck and have a good flight." The Captain said as he faded away into the night.

I stared at the spot where he disappeared for a few moments when I felt a tug on my arm. I glanced over at Rose as she tugged once more and pointed down toward the start of the tree line we had left awhile ago. "Uhm Cassie I think there are some lights down there and we need to go, can the Captain show us where this ship is or what?" she said in a whisper.

I looked over at the edge of the trees and sure enough, I could see lights moving back and forth between the foliage, "Yeah, follow me," I whispered back and led her into the side of the ship. Yeah, I know I should have told her the Captain wasn't with us anymore, but no sense in letting her worry about something she couldn't change.

Moving back down the side of the ship was a lot easier outside than it was on the inside. There were tubes and wires and all kinds of equipment strewn across the passageway. Luckily the top half of the ship had huge gaping holes in it and what little light that came through lit up the interior of the ship because we sure weren't going to use any lights with aliens outside.

Rose and I were really starting to feel the fatigue from the long climb up the mountain and trying to negotiate our way around the ship's passageway when we came to an area of darkness. The last opening ripped in the ship's upper hull had been around a bend in the passageway we had been following and now we were in an area where we had to hold onto each other's hands or we would lose each other in the night.

"Now what do we do?" Rose whispered in my ear.

"Now we need light to see where we are," I said as I reached to the side of my pack and pulled out a small torch light. I felt along the bottom of the light and found the dial that controlled the brightness and turned the setting as low as it would go before I flicked the on button.

"Okay listen, Rose, I've got us light, but since it is very small and dim, watch your step," I said.

As the light barely lit up the night before us, I could see it glow off the front of something metal just two feet in front of us. It took me a few seconds to figure out that we were standing in front of the spaceship that we had been looking for.

As I stood there gaping at the ship in front of us, Rose gave my arm a shake and whispered, fear tingeing her voice. "Cassie, I think I saw a flash of light come from around the bend back there."

ROBERT WRIGHT

BOOK 2
EMMA

Emma

"Come on, let's move," I whispered back grabbing Rose's arm and sliding alongside the ship in front of us. I looked back the way we had come, but couldn't see any lights flashing, but I did hear what sounded like metal scraping on metal.

Rose gave a little start and a small squeak escaped her lips and echoed throughout the space we were in. I gave her a cross look and she mouthed back 'sorry' in silence with a shrug of her shoulders.

We waited in the silent dark with our small feeble light the only comfort given to the two of us. After a couple of minutes that seemed like years of waiting for another sound or flash of light, I turned and looked down the side of the ship that we were leaning against and thought I saw a slight indication of a hatch.

I slid my mouth as close to Rose's ear as I could and whispered to her, "Follow me and do not make another sound."

She nodded her head, but her tight grip on my arm never let up as she followed me carefully down the side of the ship. As we moved down the side, I could feel the cold metal beneath the hand that I held against the ship. I hoped that when we got into the vessel it would be in working order and that whoever this Emma was it was someone that knew how to fly us out of here.

Sure enough, about ten feet down there was a hatch, but the problem was I saw no keypad to punch in the numbers that the Captain had told me about.

"What's wrong, Cassie?" Rose whispered as I scanned the area around the hatch for some kind of keypad.

"We're supposed to punch in a number, but there is nowhere to punch it into," I said looking desperately back at Rose.

"Oh, this is so not good, Cassie," she whispered as we heard a loud thump back up the passageway and as we both looked in that direction we saw a quick flash of light in the dark.

We stood frozen, then burst out of our stupor feeling along the side of the ship for some keypad or way to open the door before us. "Here, here look at this Cassie," Rose said as she wiped the grime off the ship and a small hatch appeared.

"Great, now what?" I said as Rose pushed on the small door and it popped sideways and there before us was a keypad.

"Come on Cassie hurry, put in the number," Rose said, but my hand was already reaching for the numbers to punch in the code the Captain had given me. The ship's door slid open and I pushed Rose inside as I glanced down the passageway and now saw several lights moving toward us.

I hopped in next to my cousin and looked over at her standing there with wide eyes. "Damn! Now how do we close it?"

With no warning, the door silently zipped shut and a light lit up, blinding us for a second with its brightness after the darkness outside. "Uhm, did you do that, Cassie?"

"Nope, I was hoping you did."

"Hello, Commander Cassie, it is so nice to have you back."

We both jumped and then looked over at a speaker in the wall that this new voice issued from. "Uhm, you heard a voice too didn't you, Rose?"

"Oh, yeah, I heard it too, why?"

"Oh just checking, Rose, to make sure that it wasn't a ghost I was hearing."

"No problem, Cassie, but if that was a ghost then I think I'm hearing them now."

"Who's there?" I asked the speaker, feeling silly talking to the wall of the ship.

"Commander Cassie, you know that it is I – Emma."

"Uhm I'm sorry, but I am not Commander Cassie, I'm just Cassie. The Commander, from my understanding, was my great- great something grandmother."

"Oh," the voice said with some puzzlement. *"Then that explains why you look so young for being one hundred and eighty years old, and why you look so much shorter."*

Rose sniggered behind her hand as I stomped my foot down on the deck of the ship. "Listen to me, I'm not that short so get off my case will you?"

"I am very sorry Cassie that is not the Commander, but who is the other human that I detect standing next to you please?"

"Rose, my name is Rose, and where are you, Emma?"

"Hello Rose, but what do you mean 'where are you?' Why I am right here, of course."

"Uhm Emma, what Rose is saying is that we hear you, but we cannot see you so where are you sitting right now?"

"Oh, I am sorry, my dears, I think I see the problem now. No one has told you who I am, have they?"

"No, they haven't, all they have said was that once we got to the ship you would take us off this planet and away from the aliens that are chasing us, and help me find my parents."

There was silence in the air as though Emma was

processing the information I had laid on her. *"Alright, my dears, I need to tell you that I am Emma and that Emma is the name that my maker gave me."*

"Maker, maker of what?" Rose asked with puzzlement in her voice.

I stood there looking at the speaker and then around me at the ship and thought oh damn. "Uhm Emma? Are you the ship?"

Rose looked at me as though I had grown a second head and then her mouth dropped to her chin as Emma answered me, *"Why yes, Cassie sweetie, I am the ship and my makers named me Emma."*

"Oh, I see now," Rose said as she looked around at the ship as I had.

"Well, now that we have that figured out Emma can you take us away from the aliens that are chasing us on this planet?"

"Well, of course, dears, I can do that. You don't think I would let some old nasty aliens take the descendants of Commander Cassie, did you?"

"Oh okay, then when can we leave Emma?"

"Leave? Why we have been in space since I detected the aliens entering the hanger bay where I was housed and you walked in. Of course, in the haste of our departure, I may have incinerated those same aliens, hope you dears do not have any problems with that?"

"Wait! You mean we are in space? No way," Rose said in awe.

I stood there in shock thinking that we hadn't even felt anything so there could be no way that we were where Emma said we were. "Uhm Emma not that I don't believe you, but can we see that we are where you say we are?"

"Why of course my dears, follow this passageway to the front of the ship and I will show you that we are indeed where I told you we were."

So Rose and I followed the passageway to the front of the ship. We passed several small rooms that had beds set into the wall and not much else. Then we came upon a small kitchen unit that made the one on Moe's boat look huge, and then we were in a control room that had four chairs each arranged around separate panels.

"Now, my dears, if you would be so kind as to dump those packs you are carrying on the floor and take the pilot and co-pilot chairs I will show you that we are indeed in space."

So Rose and I did what Emma asked and dumped our packs and each of us took a seat at the front of the ship. Guess when the ship asks nicely it is only polite to do what she wants. "Okay now what, Emma?"

"Why now this, dears," Emma said as the front of the ship above the panel opened up and Rose and I were looking out at stars that we had never in our life seen before. *"So believe me now, my dears, that we are indeed in space?"*

I heard Rose whisper something next to me, but it was so

low that I wasn't exactly sure what she had said. I glanced over at her wide-eyed stare and knew that I probably looked close to the same myself.

"Oh I believe you Emma, but just where are we and what about the aliens, don't they have their own spaceship that can get us?" I asked still looking out at the stars in front of us with awe.

"Well for your first question, Cassie, we are hiding behind one of a handful of small moons that orbit this planet. For your second question, there is indeed an alien ship out there. I detected it as we took off from that mountain, but I took countermeasures that will not allow them to find us, so don't worry we are perfectly safe," Emma said with some satisfaction in her voice.

"Well, I have some more questions, Emma," I said.

"And I do too," Rose said in between a couple of yawns that had my body answering with echoes of my own.

"Listen, my dears, my sensors tell me that you two are basically at the end of your human stamina. I would suggest that you get refreshed, eat and catch some sleep while I keep watch over you. I promise that there is no way that the aliens will find us and that I will wake you if any emergency happens."

Rose and I looked over at each other and she shrugged her shoulders at me as though to say that the decision was up to me. Well so far in our short encounter Emma had not steered us wrong so what the hell. "Okay, Emma where can we get refreshed at?"

"Why that is easy, sweeties, see that door behind you? That is the refreshment room, and I am sure that you have seen the galley and bedrooms when you came from the hatch to the control room, right?"

Rose and I stood up and opened the door that Emma told us about and saw that the refreshment room was as small as the rest of the ship. "I'll tell you what, Rose, you get cleaned up and I'll try to get us some food together," I said as I headed back to the cooking area.

"Okay thanks, Cassie. I won't be long, promise," Rose said as she grabbed her pack up and hopped into the refreshment room sliding the door closed behind her.

I took the short walk down the passageway and stepped into the galley when the smell of food wafted on the air. I looked over at the cooking unit and saw that there wasn't anything going and wondered where those wonderful smells were coming from. "Uhm Emma what's cooking and where?"

"Sorry, my hon, I took the liberty of making you a meal while your cousin cleans up. The meal is cooking in my internal area. The set up in front of you is in case the crew decides to do their own cooking, but on long patrols or when we are in battle situations, I can provide all needed nourishment for the crew," Emma said with a little annoying tone of satisfaction creeping into her voice.

"Well thanks, Emma, you sure are efficient, aren't you?"

"Well yes I am hon, I was state of the art one hundred and fifty years ago, Cassie."

Then Rose walked in wearing a blue jumpsuit with soft dark blue boots and looked at the speaker set in the wall of the kitchen unit with a puzzled look. "Uhm Emma were you talking to Cassie at the same time you were talking to me?"

"Oh why yes, my dears, I am tasked to complete multiple duties at the same time with different crew members so that I can carry on conversations with up to five different humans on and off this ship if the humans have a communication set."

"Oh okay well, thanks, Emma; thought I was losing my mind there for a second," Rose said as she looked over at the empty cook area and then sniffed the air. "Well, maybe I am losing my mind because I smell something good. You couldn't have cooked it did you, Cassie?" Rose asked wrinkling her nose at me

I huffed at my cousin's lack of appreciation of my cooking and grabbed up my pack to hit the refresher. "It's Emma's doing, you'll have to ask her where the food is. I'm going to get a quick clean up so save me some food, cousin." See if I cook for her next time she is hungry, I thought. Man because you give someone food poisoning one time they never let you forget it.

I heard both of them say something, but my mind was on getting out of these grubby clothes and then a hot meal, but the sleep part of the ship's plan was going to have to wait until we got all of our questions answered.

The refresher room was tiny with just the basics, a small

toilet, a sink that folded down over the toilet and a stall that I took was the shower. I stripped down to my underwear and looked around for a place to throw my dirty clothes when a voice sounded behind me making me jump in the air. *"Throw that nasty stuff in that little door there to your right, dear."*

I looked over and saw a small door pop open and threw my clothes into it. *"Now your underthings too, hon,"* Emma's voice sounded again from the wall.

"Uhm Emma a little privacy if you don't mind?" I said looking up at the speakers.

"I'm sorry dear, but my makers didn't allow me to do that."

"Fine Emma then how do you use this shower," I said a little crossly as I stripped out of the undergarments that had long needed to be cleaned and stepped into the shower.

"It is very simple, sweetie. This shower uses light energy to clean you off like this," and as Emma said that, I felt waves of energy passing over my body, first a bright white light that seemed to energize me and then a blue light that I could swear left behind a smell of jasmine in the air.

"There you go, hon, all done," Emma said as a red light passed over me that left my whole body tingling from head to toe.

"Yeah, thanks, Emma, sorry about sounding a little grumpy before, but I like my privacy every once and awhile, so this will take a little getting used to.

"Oh that is alright my dear, now get dressed, because I am serving lunch now." I reached down for my pack for some clothes, but a different panel next to the one that I threw my dirty stuff in opened up and out slid a matching outfit like Rose's.

"Uhm you do know that we have our own clothes, Emma, don't you?"

"Oh yes that little sweetie Rose told me that, but hon these are so much more practical of an outfit to wear when you are onboard a ship, don't you think? That way you can save your own clothes for when you are planet side, and besides the color so fits you and your cousin's eyes."

"Okay, Emma you win," I said as the smell of food drifted through the door of the refresher. I dressed in a hurry as my stomach growled at me all the way back to the galley. I guess it was trying to tell me that it had been a while since I had fed it.

Rose was once more dishing up two full bowls of whatever smelled so good by the time I hit the door of the galley. "Oh, there you are, Cassie. Here take this and we can go sit up front since there doesn't seem to be any chairs around here," she said as she looked around her and then headed out the door to the forward part of the ship.

As we sat down in the chairs we had occupied before to eat our meal, a slow soft melody started to play out of Emma's speaker. It wasn't like anything I had heard before, but I liked the music that filled the air. "Emma, what is this music, I don't think I have heard it before?"

"Oh sorry, my dears, my makers said that this kind of music during meals would be soothing to humans. I can change it to something else if you prefer."

"NO, NO," both Rose and I yelled at the same time.

"It's fine Emma, I just never heard anything like this before," I said, sitting back in my chair and listening to the haunting music that flowed around us.

"No problem, dear, this music is some old recordings from Earth. Now if you two are done with your food, why don't you put them on the tray in front of you?"

  I was going to ask what tray when a panel in front of us once again popped open and a tray slid out. Rose and I put our empty bowls on the tray and poof they disappeared behind the panel. A girl could get used to service like this, I thought.

"Now it is nap time, my dears," Emma said once the panel shut. *"Lay back and let the lullaby soothe you."*

"Emma, we don't want to sleep," I said as I sat up and grabbed the sides of the chairs to haul myself out of it.

"Oh that's okay, dears, but I know what is best and the two of you need sleep." As Emma said this, I heard a small hiss coming from above us and I slumped back into my chair, my arms now unable to pull my weight up from its soft surface.

As my eyes fought to keep open I could feel the chair straighten out so that I was soon laying flat on my back. I fought whatever Emma had sprayed on us, but I knew it was a losing battle as I sunk down into the depths of the music that was still softly playing and succumbed to the night.

Questions and Answers

I came awake from the dreamless deep sleep that Emma had put us under, really, really peeved at this ship. How dare she do that to us, I thought. "EMMA! What did you do and how long have I been asleep?" Next to me in her own chair, I could see that Rose was now stirring awake either on her own or because of my loud protest.

"What happened, Cassie?" Rose mumbled as she rubbed the sleep out of her eyes and looked over at me in puzzlement.

"EMMA?" I said once again, my anger going up another notch since she seemed to be ignoring me altogether now.

"No need to be cross, dearest. I did what was best for you and sweet Rose."

I took a deep breath to calm myself down enough so that I could have a conversation and hopefully get some information out of the ship we were in. "Fine. Sorry for yelling, but we told you that we didn't want to sleep, that we wanted answers, Emma."

"Fine hon," Emma said with some petulance in her voice. *"Go get the meal I have waiting for you in the galley and when you come back I will answer all your questions."*

"Uhm we just ate, Emma; didn't we?" Rose asked.

"Well sweeties you have been asleep for eight hours so I thought you might be hungry. I mean I can dispose of the food if you want?"

I looked over at Rose and she shrugged her shoulders like she seemed to be doing a lot lately and left the decision up to me again. I sat there for a second thinking, but the smell that was swimming down the passageway made my stomach growl and roll so once more it won out and I got up and headed toward the galley. "No, no Emma we will go get the food, thanks," I said to the ship.

We once again scooped up the great food that Emma had prepared into bowls without saying a word and headed back to the control room of the ship. As we sat down, Rose sniffed the food in her bowl and then a look of concern crossed her face. "Uhm Emma you have been in that same spot for one hundred and some years right?'

"Yes, dear exactly one hundred and fifty years, three days, 10 hours, and. . ."

"Okay, okay Emma I got that, but the question is, is this food we are eating, I mean is it that old and is it safe to eat if it's over a hundred and some years old?"

"Oh, you don't have to worry about that, hon. For you see, I don't carry real food. I process food and water out of, let's say stuff or residue produced on the ship while in space."

"Oh," we both whispered at the same time as we each put ours bowls down on the control panel. I looked over at Rose who looked as green as I felt.

"Now eat up my dears, this food was stuff that I collected from the area around the main ship and we won't need to go into the process I told you about for some time."

"Uhm and what kind of stuff did you collect around the main ship, Emma?" I asked as both Rose and I picked up our bowls and started to dig into our meal once more.

"No, no don't tell us that. I don't want to know; I want to finish this without knowing what I'm eating," Rose said between mouthfuls of her food.

"Cassie, do you still want to know?"

"Uhm no Emma that's okay, Rose is right I don't need to know that or when or if you change over to processing food in space from our stuff."

"Well okay sweeties, now you have questions for me?"

"Yeah, Emma, first though are we still safe and in the same place?"

"Oh, of course, hon, if for any reason there had been any dangers from the aliens or anything else I would have woke the both of you, trust

me."

"Yeah, well when you stop putting us to sleep against our wishes, then I will trust you, Emma."

There was silence for a few seconds before Emma responded. *"Now sweeties don't you feel more awake and up to hearing the answers to your questions with a clear head? My only concern is for the well-being of the two of you."*

"Fine Emma, we'll table that discussion for later, but for now have the aliens detected where we are?" I asked.

"No hon, those little buggers could never find me if they tried, and believe me they are trying hard right now."

"Okay, then I'll take your word for that Emma . . ."

"Why thank you hon, you don't know how much that means to me."

Rose and I shot each other a quick glance, each of us not sure if a ship was supposed to act and sound like this at all. She was starting to sound a little scary, almost like some of those old ladies on Ecstasy that always seemed to mother everyone they came in contact with no matter if they were family or not.

"Uhm Emma what are you exactly?" I asked, hoping that I was not offending the ship, for it would be a long cold walk back to the planet below if she got mad and kicked us out.

"Oh, my dears why I am or I should say I was the newest state of the art long range patrol ship for Earth. This was supposed to be me and

my sister's maiden voyage before we ran into the aliens and all the trouble that came with it."

"You had a sister?" Rose said.

"Oh yes, but she was a little different from me. She was an older model and my maker had not added her little touches to her like she did with me. Actually, just between you and me, I really do think I was the smarter of the two of us, but don't tell her that."

"Uhm Emma we won't tell her, but where is she?" I asked.

"Oh she was in the other hanger bay, dearies, but it was funny that I could never connect with her after the crash. That's why I think I am the smarter of the two of us."

"Oh, I'm sorry Emma, but we were told that the other ship in the hanger bay was destroyed in the crash."

In the quiet that ensued, we could hear the air moving through the vents for several seconds before Emma spoke again. *"Oh I see so then I was the only one of my kind to survive on the ship?"* Her voice seeped out of the speakers in a low whisper. If I hadn't known she was a ship and not a human I would have sworn that I could hear her voice tearing up.

"Yes, I think so Emma and both of us are really sorry for your loss," Rose whispered back to the ship.

"Thank you, hons, for letting me know about Sara. Now where were we? Oh yes, I am a long range patrol ship that can hold a crew of four but up to six in an emergency. Of course, then it can get awful crowded in here and it can tax my systems a bit."

"Well, Emma if you were a long range patrol ship then what were you and your sister doing on the Captain's ship?" I asked

"Well you see, sweetie, we had been on our final shakedown cruise and were headed back to Earth when the Captain heard about the aliens and went to rescue his wife and as many people as he could."

"How long were you on the Captain's ship, Emma?"

"Oh well, let's see I think we were assigned to that ship for five years for testing."

"That seems like an awfully long time to test two ships, Emma."

"Yes, well it seems that for some reason the testing got a little skewed and the Captain and Commander Cassie had to find out what the problem was."

"Did they ever figure out what the problem was with the tests?" Rose asked.

"Uhm, no?" Emma said with an electronic chuckle.

"Emma, do you know why the tests had problems?" I asked, not liking a chuckle from a ship, something was not right here.

"Well, of course, I know what was wrong, my dears," Emma said with what I thought was a sly little giggle, and when a ship giggles and you are in deep space you worry.

"And?" both Rose and I said at the same time.

"Oh well, sweeties, you see I thought that the Captain and Commander Cassie were perfect together so I messed with the tests so that I could get the two of them to fall in love and live happily ever after."

You could hear a pin drop in the control room as both Rose and I looked at each other in shock. Great, I thought, we were in the hands of one crazy ship and we had no place to go except into the cold reaches of space.

"Uhm Emma what did your sister think of all this?" I asked.

"Oh well, you see I am different from my sister. When my maker made me she was dying and I was her last project, so she went and transferred her personality into my brain center."

"Oh," was all I could say for a second thinking that that explained Emma's strange behavior and the way that she talked to Rose and me.

"Oh, my dears I think now I know what the problem is, you probably thought that I was some crazy out of control ship that had kidnapped you and took in into space to do all kinds of naughty things to you."

"Oh no of course not, Emma," I said shaking my head back and forth.

"Perish the thought," Rose said shaking her head back and forth even harder than I was.

"Well, that's good, dearies, because I will have you know that my maker was very sane when she gave me her personality."

"Oh well that is good to hear Emma, but uhm why would you go and try to hook up the Captain and the Commander like you did?" I asked, curious about the ship's motives.

"Well like I said, my dears, the Captain and the Commander were so perfect for each other and I was so bored with the tests that they wanted us to do."

"Okay, I guess I can see that Emma, but I'm curious what kind of tests were you having done on you and why?"

"Well, my dears, that is confidential information, but since you are such nice girls I will tell you. You see my sister and me were special one of a kind ships. My maker and her people had found a way to fit all the engines, weapons, and life support of a capital battleship into our platform."

"How did your maker do that and was that a battleship we were on?" I asked looking around at the small ship we were in and thinking of how big the main ship had been.

"Oh no, sweeties," Emma's laugh screeched out of her speakers. *"That little ship we were on was only a cruiser, a battleship is about ten times the size of the Captain's ship, and my maker discovered how to miniaturize all my components."*

"Well that's fine, but it still should take more than four or five people to run all these systems, shouldn't it Emma?"

"Well yes you would think so," Emma said with another laugh that caused Rose and me to cover our ears. *"Sorry about that, dears, but the reason that we can function so efficiently is that with our AI brains we can run everything on our platforms without any human*

intervention at all. At the time, our AI intelligence was the most gifted thing ever made."

"So you don't really need us at all do you, Emma?" I asked.

"Why of course I need you, my dears, I have been so lonely for the last one hundred and fifty years," Emma said with a sob that came over her speaker.

"Well don't worry, Emma, we are here now so you won't be lonely, okay?" Rose said after she looked over at me with these sad soft eyes of hers. She always was picking up orphaned or hurt animals when she was younger and trying her best to nurse them back to health.

"Yeah, what she said, Emma, I guess we aren't going anywhere anytime soon," I said.

"Well, that is so nice of you girls to befriend such an old gal like me. Now we need to put our heads together to figure out what you little sweeties want to do."

"Can we help the humans down on the planet and destroy the aliens, Emma?' I asked.

"Oh well, I am afraid to tell you that all humans down on the planet have been terminated."

"All of them? But how about the Tekis, did the aliens, uhm, terminate them too?"

"No, my dears the aliens seemed to have left the Teki alone in that they pose no threat to their race due to the fact that they do not possess

space travel."

"So, Emma, is that why the aliens attacked the outer rim worlds; because we had space travel?"

"Yes, dear, that and that we were encroaching on what they considered their territory."

"Well, how come they didn't ask us to leave? Why kill so many people?"

"Well you see, my dears, it seems that the Captain and Commander discovered that we had found the aliens years ago and that some in our government decided that we needed the space more than the aliens. So they wiped out some settlements on the outer rim planets and then brought in our own people. At least that is what the Captain and Commander thought."

"But why would someone do that, Emma?"

"If they did it, sweetie, it is because space on Earth is at a premium and the leaders needed planets to send the overflow to. I am sorry to say that Earth was not all flowers and sunlight. It was very crowded and nations fought nations for space, food, and who ruled who."

"Oh well, Emma, I still think that, if possible, we should get back to Earth. I mean it was over a hundred and fifty years ago that Earth was like that, I'm sure it must have changed by now, don't you think?"

"I am sorry to say, my dears, that the probabilities of the changes you are thinking of are minuscule at best, but if it is your wish to go to Earth we can do that," Emma said, the sadness leaking through the

speaker. It was surprising how much emotion she was able to convey to us.

Rose and I looked at each other each with our own thoughts flowing through our heads. "Well, what do you think we should do, Cassie? It's not like we can hang out here in space forever."

"Yeah, you're right," I said thinking that since there were no more humans on the planet that the aliens had got rid of my parents too. "If nothing else we should let Earth know that there are still aliens out here looking for the home world."

"So then I take it you want to go to Earth then, my dears?"

"Yeah, Emma, I guess that we should do that since we have no one here for either one of us," I said as I got up from my chair to find a place to be alone for a few minutes to wallow in self-pity.

"Uhm Cassie, my dear, perhaps I should have said something earlier, but I said there were no humans on the planet, but there are two life forms on one of the alien's ships."

I stood there and looked at the speaker in front of me and counted to ten, for such a smart ship Emma could be frustrating sometimes in her answers. "Can you tell, Emma, if they are my parents and which ship that they are on?"

"Yes, my dear, I can tell you that the two humans are on the alien command ship, but I will need to hook up to one of their ships to tell for sure who the humans are."

Rose and I once more stared at each other for a few seconds before I asked. "Okay and just how can we get close enough to a ship to find out who is on the command ship, Emma?"

"Oh well, that is easy, my dears, like I said before we have the technology to not been seen by any ships out in space. So then we sneak up to one of their small scout ships, take over the crew and then hook up to their computer and there you go – we find out who is on the command ship, sweeties."

Throwing Rocks

I couldn't believe that we were doing this. After Emma told us how we could discover who the humans were on the command ship, we were soon closing in on the alien scout ship Rose and I would take over.

"I don't think that this is going to work, Emma," Rose said with some fright tingeing her voice.

"Oh please, hon, you'll see how easy this is; there will be no problems at all."

"Yeah, no problems, except for the aliens," Rose answered, the sarcastic tone of her voice bouncing off the walls of the ship.

I looked at the speaker that Emma's voice flowed through and was worried, like my cousin, that Emma's plan wasn't as foolproof as she thought it was. "Listen, Emma, what happens if the crew gets a signal off to the command ship?"

"They won't get a signal off, my dears; because as soon as we touch

ships together I will jam their communications and you two go in and take out the crew. Like I said, no problem."

I looked down at the radar scope that I sat in front of and watched as we closed the distance to the alien's ship. Emma had picked a scout ship that was stationed on the other side of Ecstasy from the main group. We had looped around the outer planets in the system and approached our intended target on a vector that would keep us well away from all the other ships in orbit.

Emma said we could have come straight in from where we had been hiding, but Rose and I weren't that confident about the ship's ability to stay hidden from the aliens and we begged her to take the longer route to the ship.

"Now my dears we are one hundred feet from the alien ship and holding. I need you to go to the airlock and wait until I engage with them."

"Uhm Emma how do we get them to open up for us? It's not like we can knock on the door and ask for a cup of sugar or something," I said.

"Oh, you silly thing you don't have to worry because we aren't going through their airlock. I am going to blow a hole through the side of their ship and you two will go through and kill any aliens that are still alive. Right now I register four life forms on that ship. So now off you go and please be careful, sweeties. I would hate for one of you to get shot and mess up your new outfits. Red does so clash with blue, you know."

With that cheerful thought, Rose and I headed down the passageway toward the airlock, Rose muttering under her breath about Emma's priorities the whole way. When we got there we found a small open panel with two slimmer blaster rifle designs than we had used on the planet below us.

"Here you go, my dears, these will be easier to handle and have more power than those old antiques you had planet side."

"Uhm thanks, Emma, but aren't these antiques too if they are over one hundred years old?" I said grabbing up one of the rifles and giving it a quick look over.

"Yes dear they may be over a hundred years old but at the time, they were the newest design in weapons made for shipboard use. Only the best for you, my honeys, to kill those nasty aliens."

"Yeah, thanks," Rose echoed as she followed my lead. "Uhm anything we need to know about these weapons?"

"Oh not much dears, just push those red buttons on the side and small red dots will flash out the front; put a dot on the target and pull the trigger. It's really simple – point, pull, and one dead alien."

"I don't know, Emma, if this is going to work."

"Oh but I know, hon, remember to follow my directions on the com gear I gave you," Emma said as we heard a clunk outside the ship and then an explosion right outside the airlock. *"Now, dears you are down to three crewmembers on the alien's ship."*

With that the airlock opened and Rose and I could see

what had happened to the one alien that got caught up in the middle of Emma's knock, knock on the side of their ship. I could see pieces of ship and alien mixed all up and down the passageway and spread all over the bulkheads.

I stepped into the passageway and looked left then was turning to the right as I heard Emma's urgent voice in my ear, *"Kneel and shoot right, Cassie."*

I saw a flash of light pass over my head as I kneeled and as I pressed the trigger of my rifle, a red dot reflected off of the center of an alien's body. Then a second later it was replaced by a fist-sized sizzling hole in which I could see through to the bulkhead behind it.

"Very good, sweetie, now you are down to two crewmembers. Cassie, please go to your right toward the front of the ship and Rose please go left to the aft of the ship."

I stepped forward looking down the passageway toward the right so that my cousin could step out into the passageway behind me. I looked over my shoulder at her and nodded. "Keep your eyes open and shoot first."

"Yeah, same you to Cassie and good luck," Rose said as she then headed down the passageway leading aft.

"Oh, my dears, don't be silly. You don't need luck when you have me," Emma chuckled in our ears.

I moved down the passageway, stepping over the body of the alien I had shot avoiding the bits of insides that were splattered along the bulkhead of the ship when I heard

Emma's voice once again. *"Stop Rose, there is one life form right around the next hatch, please do as I say and press that blue button next to the red. Yes, that one dear, now press the trigger and then duck down."*

From behind me, I heard a thump and then another explosion. "Rose," I yelled back toward the way that my cousin had gone.

"Oh she is perfectly fine, my dear, and you are now down to one crewmember, which unfortunately now knows exactly where you are because you yelled."

"Yeah, sorry Emma I guess I'm new at this whole highjacking alien ships and killing them stuff."

"No problem, hon, do try to remember that they are out to kill you and will not hesitate to do so without question."

I slowly moved forward until I came to a closed hatch that I assumed led to the alien control area. "Okay, now what Emma?" I said looking at the barrier and wondering how we would get through it.

"Oh, no problem my dear, just give me a second to reroute their life-support system and there the door should open now."

I had just enough time to bring my weapon up and press the trigger as the door popped aside and an alien moved as though to go through it, but unfortunately, for him, he was thrown backward with a fist-sized hole in his middle like the one I had shot earlier.

"There my dears, now you have no more aliens to worry about."

I turned at the sound of feet moving and looked at my cousin who was a little green around the edges but sported a small smile none the less. "Be careful of the blue button, Cassie, it shoots some small explosive and can pack a little bit of a kickback," she said rotating the arm that the rifle had rested against.

I nodded wishing that hopefully we wouldn't have any more problems or reasons to use these weapons again. "Now what should we do, Emma?"

"Oh give me a second to clear out the air and then you can click in that interface I gave you into their computer and hopefully it will download all the info we need about these guys."

"What did you do to the air in there, Emma? I thought we were here to find out who the humans were on the Command ship."

"Well for your first question, sweeties, I rerouted engine coolant into the control room vents and that is why alien opened the door, and there now it is cleared out."

"You can do that?" Rose asked.

"Yes dear, I can tap into their weapons, and life-support systems from here, but I need to be physically connected to their ship to get into the command computer systems. As for your second question, we may need to learn all we can to rescue whoever those two humans are on the Command ship."

"Okay, okay Emma I see your point, now where do we connect you so you can get into the computer."

"Okay dears, I am sorry I if I sounded a little snippy, but I worry about you two. Now go into the control room and on the front most panel you will see a plug-in where you can put the interface."

Rose and I walked into the control room, trying not to look at the alien that I had put a hole through. Stepping over its body we came to the control panel that Emma told us about and we both looked down at it in disgust.

"Uhm, sweeties, is there a problem over there, can't you find the interface connect?"

"Oh, we found it, Emma," I said as Rose and I glanced at each other and then back down at the mess in front of us. "It's just that when I shot that last alien it seems that his insides splattered all over the interface and control panel."

"Oh, I see hon, well uhm it does need to be cleaned off to work."

"Really, no kidding Emma?" I said with as much sarcasm as I could put into my voice. "Give us a second, Emma, we may be used to shooting aliens now but we're not used to cleaning alien guts off of ship parts."

"Alright hon, but I must inform you that we only have three hours to complete the data transfer and to get out of here."

Rose and I once more glanced at each other as we found some material in a cabinet and started to clean alien guts off the area we needed to use. "And why only three hours,

Emma?"

"Well, my dears, we only have three hours because that is how long we have before the other alien ships arrive at this point and I would like to be gone and have this ship destroyed well before then."

"Uhm Emma, I thought you said that there would only be one scout ship on this side of the planet and that all the rest would stay with the command ship, you did say that right?"

"Uhm why yes, dears, I did say that but if we just stand here and worry about all my faults and failures, which of course is a very short list, we won't get done what we came here to do."

"Right," I said as I finished wiping down the control panel in front of us. Pulling the interface that Emma had said she would need to connect to the alien ship's computer out of my side pocket, I plugged it into the hole that matched the end of the interface. "There, is it working?" I asked.

"Oooh yes there we go baby, come to momma," Emma cooed in a voice I never hope to hear from her again.

"Uhm Emma?"

"Oh, sorry dears just got a little carried away there for a second it has been awhile since I interfaced with another computer and it feels oh so good. Now you two sweeties run along back to the ship and get ready for a fast getaway."

Rose and I didn't waste any time waiting around or questioning Emma as we ran through the ship hopping over dead aliens and finally getting back to the airlock of our ship. "Okay we are in Emma, now what?"

"Yes, I know hon, put away your weapons and come to the control room."

So, of course, Rose and I did what Emma had told us to do. I almost felt like I was back home and having my momma tell what to do for my weekend chores once again. "Okay, now what, Emma?" I said as we both entered the control room.

"My, my, my dears you are so full of questions today, aren't you? But for now, you can sit down in your chairs and buckle up for in about fifteen minutes we may have a bumpy ride."

"Emma, did you get all the info from the alien's ship that you wanted?" I asked.

"Yes I did dear and I can tell you that the two humans aboard the command ship are indeed your parents . . ."

"Yeah, great, now all we need to do is get my parents off of the command ship and head to Earth."

"Uhm, well, there may be a slight problem with that idea, Cassie dear."

"There's no problem, Emma, let's do what we did with this ship and then bug out of here with my parents, see no problem at all."

"Well see there two small problems, one is that the command ship that your parents are on is about thirty times the size of this scout ship. So

it would not be a stroll in the park like it was with this ship. Second, the reason these other scout ships are moving in our direction is to make sure that the skies are clear for them and the command ship to head home."

"And you know all this because why?" I asked.

"I know this, my dear, because their computer told me all this. Now sweeties please sit down and buckle up for we are going to make our little takeover look like an accident."

We both sat down and buckled down into our seats as I could feel Emma disengage from the alien ship. My eyes went wide as I saw out the front window that Emma had headed us out toward some asteroids clustered out near us.

"Uhm Emma, what are you doing?" I asked knowing that I would probably not like the answer.

"Why, my dears, I am going to catch one of these itty, bitty rocks and then smash it into the alien ship you were on."

"And you are going to do this how and why, Emma?" Rose asked because I was totally shocked by the ship's answer and really didn't want to take this line of questioning any further than it had gone so far.

"The how will be easy dears, I will simply pull one of these rocks along with the tractor beam in my tail and then we will swing around and smash it into the alien's ship. The why is because when the rock hits the ship there will be a glorious light show and nothing left for their friends to find."

"Uhm won't the aliens know something is up?"

"Remember dears they can't see me so all they will see is their ship crash into a floating rock and assume that the crew messed up, happens all the time in space dears, so no worries."

"Yeah, let's try not to let it happen to us," I muttered under my breath watching as Emma swung around in front of one of the asteroids and then headed back toward the alien ship gaining speed the closer she got to it.

"What was that dear, I didn't catch what you said?"

"Oh, nothing Emma, nothing at all," I said with a giggle, and then glanced over at Rose who had a large smile plastered all over her face. Oops, guess Emma had heard me as Rose shook her head and then winked at me.

"Here we go, my dears," Emma said as we whipped past the alien ship and then turned forward so that we were now accelerating away from it. As I felt the ship pick up speed I could see the rock that Emma had been towing slam into the alien ship at full speed on a view screen in front of us. Emma had been right about one thing, it was a spectacular light show as the ship and rock met in space and in a blink of an eye they both disappeared in a large flash.

I could feel Emma stop and we watched as whatever little pieces that were left of the ship and rock slowly dissipated into the dark of space. I looked down at the clock on the panel in front of me and saw that about an hour had expired and figured we had about two hours to kill before the next alien ships would be within range of us.

Revenge

Rose and I sat for the next hour watching the scout ships move toward where their companions had turned into so much cosmic dust and debris. Emma had suggested that we each take the time to get into the refreshment cabinet and grab some food during the wait.

While Rose was getting cleaned up, I sat there watching the slow movement of the alien ships and wondered why they were taking so long to cover the same distance that we had covered in what seemed like a blink of an eye.

"Uhm Emma, I got a question for you."

"Yes dear, what is it?"

"How come it's taking these guys so long to get here?"

"Well you see, sweetie, these aliens, for being so smart in some ways, still use an old reactor drive in their ships. The scouts we see now can only move so fast and are only for intersystem use. The command ship has a sort of warp drive technology that they use to go from one system to the next."

"Okay, then what kind of drive do you have?"

"Why dear the original ship we were on had the same drive as the aliens, but our maker had given us a new drive that allows us to wrap space and time so that we move a lot faster. In fact, the further we are from planets the more we can wrap space and the quicker we can go."

"So it's easier for you to wrap space away from planets?"

Emma was quiet for a few seconds then I could hear a small electronic sigh sound from her speaker. *"No dear, it's not that it would be easier in that it would be safer for the planet. For if we used the full ability to wrap space and we were near a planet, we would create a temporary black hole in the area for just a millisecond, but it would be enough to destroy any planet."*

"Oh, yeah, I guess I could see where that would be bad."

"Yes, hon, that would be very bad for the planet we were near, in fact, it was suggested that these long range ships be used for that purpose."

I thought I had a pretty good idea what Emma was saying, but I wanted her to spell it out. "What exactly do you mean, Emma?"

"Oh, sweetie, I think you know exactly what I mean. It was suggested to my maker that these ships be used to find the alien's home world and we use our abilities to destroy them."

"And what did your maker think about this idea, Emma?"

"At first, my maker was against the idea, but as more of the outer rim worlds where taken over by the aliens, she knew that it was down

to the point of them or us, so that we were all programmed with the idea that should the opportunity present itself we would destroy the alien's home world."

I sat there thinking over what Emma had told me and thought I could almost hear some reluctance in her voice to carry out these orders. "Emma, if you get the chance to do this what are you going to do?"

"I find, my dear, that I am torn between looking at the two sides of this issue. The aliens did not start this war, even though I do not agree with the way that they are wiping out innocent humans that were not part of the problem."

"Yeah, from what little my parents have taught me about history, it seems like the little guy is the one that gets stepped on, not the ones that cause the problem in the first place."

"Yes that is true dear, now why don't you finish your dinner for that other sweetie is done and you need to get cleaned up for the scouts will be in range within an hour."

"Yeah, no problem, Emma," I said as Rose stepped out of the small refreshment cabinet and sniffed the air in hungry anticipation of her own dinner. "It's in the galley, cousin, waiting to be served," I said as I passed her to get cleaned up and she started back toward where the great smells were wafting from.

After taking a long time getting cleaned up and relaxed, I came out to hear Rose and Emma talking but it suddenly cut out as I entered the control room. I looked at my cousin who sat in her chair looking down at the screens before her.

"Okay, what's up you two?"

"Uhm I think Emma needs to tell you, Cassie."

"Well, dear, the ships are almost within range of us and we are still undetected by them."

"Okay that's fine Emma, but why does Rose look like someone died or something, whatever it is, just spill it, Emma."

"Alright my dear, but I think you need to sit down please for this."

"EMMA!" I screamed, a sneaky suspicion creeping into my brain what Emma was going to tell me.

"I am sorry, my dear, but the human life forms on the command ship have been terminated."

"You mean terminated as in killed, Emma? Is that what you are telling me?"

"Yes, hon, I am sorry, but that is what I am saying."

"How sure are you of this, Emma?" I said in a quiet, determined voice, as I sat down in my chair and buckled myself in.

"I am sorry dear, but I am one hundred percent certain that they have been terminated."

I looked at the screen that showed the alien scouts closing in on the last position that their companion had been and my blood boiled with anger. "First please stop saying sorry, Emma, you didn't kill them. Second are all your weapons online and working?"

"Well yes dear, but why would we need them? Like I said, the aliens have not detected us so we are safe. Once they leave the area, we will head to Earth with their home planet's coordinates and let the people on Earth take care of them."

"Yeah, well, Emma, I got a better idea," I said as I glanced over to Rose who was buckling herself into her chair with a big grin on her face.

"I am sorry dear, but what idea is better than the one I came up with?"

"Oh, that is simple Emma. We are going to kick the butt of these scouts here and swing around the planet and then wipe out the rest of these aliens."

Uhm sweeties, I don't think that that would be a rational idea at all."

"What's the matter, Emma? Afraid these alien calamari could kick your butt?" Rose threw her two cents into the conversation.

"I will have you know, sweetie, that I would be able to take on ten of

these command ships without even breaking out into a sweat as it may."

With that proclamation, we felt the kick of the ship's engines as Emma took off toward the alien scouts. Rose and I glanced over at each other, a big smile plastered on each of our faces. It was about time that we were going to get some payback for all the humans these aliens had killed I thought.

"Now, dears, since you have me doing what you want against my better judgment, what is your plan?" Emma said, a little snarkiness slipping into her voice.

"Oh that's easy," I explained. "I would like to come up from behind the scouts, and dive through the last two ships and take them out. Then come up under the front two and do the same, and then wing it depending on what the other scouts do. Sound okay to you, Emma?"

"Oh yes dears, that will work fine for me. Now just to let you know, we have torpedoes forward and aft and laser cannons also forward and aft and on each side of the ship, so let me know what your preference is, dears, as we go."

"No problem Emma and thanks," I said as we swung around to come from behind and above the enemy scouts.

"You're welcome, hon. Now let's concentrate on the job in front of us. We will be in range in five minutes."

"No problem Emma, let's use laser cannons on the first two passes then see where we are at," I said as we started to close on the ships in front of us.

There was silence in the control room as Emma came up behind the last two ships. All ten ships were spread out in a line of two ships side by side moving through space in rigid order. *"Hang on, dearies, here we go,"* Emma actually whooped as she dived down toward the last two ships under us. Oh my God, we really needed to talk to her on how a spaceship should act.

We could feel the ship accelerate with speed as we slid through the dark coldness of space as the two rearmost alien ships grew larger in our view screens. Before we hit them, though, I saw several flashes of light reach out from Emma and touch each alien ship and turn them into an expanding cloud of gas that we rode through.

"Nice shot Emma, now let's take out the front two ships," I said as I could feel Emma spin and then straighten out so that we were now pointed up in the general direction of our next targets. The eight ships left took a few seconds to process that they were under attack since we were still invisible on their radars, but by that time we were once more running through the gas clouds of two more destroyed alien ships at the front of the pack.

That left six scout ships left. Two were trying to make a run for it back to the command ship while the other four were circling a certain point in space trying to figure out where the shots had come from that had destroyed four of their companions.

"Damn Cassie, what if these guys tell the command ship what is going on, they may take off?" Rose said pointing down at the ships that were running.

"Oh sorry, my dears, I forgot to tell you that I took the liberty of jamming all communications in this area."

"No problem, Emma, I guess you have been a little busy. Can we get those two ships running away before they get out of your jamming range?" I asked, watching the screen as two of the blips moved away from the battle area.

"Oh yes dear, launching torpedoes now!" Emma said with what I thought was some glee at her being able to show off her skills. I felt four small bumps and then watched as these same blips on the screen caught up to the two fleeing ships in seconds.

As each set of blips caught up to a ship, I saw a blossom of light on the screen and then nothing. "Whoa, nice shooting Emma."

"Thank you, sweetie, now brace yourself, girls," Emma said about two seconds before I felt a jolt from the right side of the ship.

"WHAT WAS THAT!" I yelled at no one in particular.

"We are taking hits on the right side from two of the aliens," Rose answered in a calm voice that seemed to break through my momentary panic.

"Emma, I thought you said they couldn't see us?"

"Working on it, hon," Emma said as I felt the ship tip up and accelerate, spin and then dive down, her lasers blasting into the two aliens that were now lying below us. We once again shot through the expanding gasses of two alien ships that were now one with the cosmos.

"Two more left Emma and they are trying to bug out to the left," Rose said looking down at the screen in front of her.

"On it, dear. Torpedoes away," Emma said as I felt four more small thumps come from the front of the ship.

Once again I watched as the two sets of lights matched up with each ship as they raced for safety. Unfortunately, for the aliens, it was a quick race that once more they lost and then the space around us was clear.

"I see no more aliens on my screen, Emma," Rose announced to us all.

"Yes, thank you, dear, the skies are clear all around us and the command ship and the rest of the scouts are still holding their position on the other side of the planet. They are trying to communicate with their scouts here and I think we have maybe an hour before they send someone to find their lost ships."

"What do we do now, Cassie?"

I sat there thinking about the crews that we had dispatched with no trouble and wondered how far we were willing to go to destroy the ships on the other side of the planet and then their home world. "Emma, what should we do?"

"If you, my dears, are still determined to destroy the command ship and then find the alien home world and destroy it, I estimate that you will have a ninety-eight percent chance of succeeding in accomplishing this."

"Rose, what do you think?" I asked, the heat of anger slowly draining from me.

"How many people are on their home world, Emma?" Rose asked.

"It is hard to tell, sweetie, but I would say a few billion at least."

Rose looked over at me. "That's a lot of dead to put on your conscience, Cassie."

"Yeah, I know, Rose, maybe it would be a good idea to head to Earth after all?"

"Uhm, sweeties, I have some new information that I hesitate to tell you, but I promised that I would be honest with the two of you."

"What is it, Emma?" both Rose and I echoed each other.

"Well, dears, it seems that there are about three hundred humans being held on the alien's home world."

"Okay, and you know this how, Emma?"

"I have finished processing all the information that we have retrieved from the alien ship's computer, hon, and this little tidbit was buried deep within it."

"Well, then we have to go and rescue them, Emma."

"That, my dear, would not be a great idea at all, and I would put the success of such a project at less than fifty percent for us."

"Emma does it say if the humans are together or where they are on the alien's home world?"

"No sorry dear, there is no way I could tell until we got to the alien's world."

"Well, then I guess we have no choice in the matter, do we?" I said.

"I guess we don't, Cassie. Emma, take us toward the command ship full speed and at battle stations, please."

"Yes, dears, I figured that that was what you would decide. Hang on girls, here we go to kick some alien butt!" Emma said as I felt a kick in the middle of my back and the ship started to accelerate toward the space where the command ship waited.

Billy

In about an hour we were around the planet and coming up on the right side of the command ship. As I looked out at the main ship, I could see small blips of light flitter around it and move back and forth around the planet below us.

"Uhm Emma, are you sure that you can destroy that thing? It looks pretty big even from here."

"Yeah, and I count over seventy scout ships flying around the area too," Rose said with some concern.

"My dears, do you still really doubt me? As I said before I could take on ten or more of those things and their scouts, and fighters."

"Fighters?" I said looking at my screen.

"Oh yes sweetie, those smaller blips on your cousin's screen are fighters. I count at least sixty of those, the rest would be scouts."

"Oh, so that's why the blips look smaller?"

"Yes hon, but don't fret, you didn't know that. But once we are done here, I will teach you all you need to know as we travel to the alien's

home world. For now, though I need you two to concentrate on the fighters. I will give Cassie control of the lasers on the right while Rose will handle lasers on the left of the ship. "

Okay, no problems Emma, then what are you going to do?"

"Oh dear, why that is easy. I am going to fly us through the fighters and attack the command ship with torpedoes."

"But I thought they couldn't see us, Emma?"

"They can't now my dears, but as soon as I set the first spread of torpedoes toward the command ship the fighters will be all over us, and unfortunately I think it may take a few runs to destroy the command ship unless, of course, I get a lucky shot in ."

We moved through the cluster of fighters and scouts that orbited around the command ship and up and down from the planet's surface. I was glad that Emma was the one doing the driving since there were times that traffic was so heavy in some areas I was shocked that we didn't hit any ships.

As we moved closer to the command ship and saw how big it was, I had this little nagging feeling deep down in the pit of my stomach that we three had taken on more than we could handle. Then I spotted a weakness in the alien ship that might help us bring it down.

"Uhm Emma, what is your plan here?"

"Well dear, I thought we would take out the engines of the command

ship and then go from there, you know wing it as you said before."

Yeah, that's what I thought she was gonna do as we came closer to the rear of the ship looming in our view. "Well just an idea, but how about we slide along the side of the ship and put some torpedoes in that big door that the scouts and fighters keep coming out of. Think that might cause damage to the ship, Emma?"

It was quiet for a second and then I heard a small electronic chuckle, *"Why, my dear, you so did inherit Commander Cassie's knack for battle."*

"Uhm thanks, I think," I said as I felt Emma change directions and then move slowly toward the open hatch that spewed the smaller ships.

As we got to a point where we were directly in front of the hatch we had been aiming for, but out of the way of the ships leaving and entering, I was looking hard to see a pattern to how long the doors were opening and closing and talking to Emma about the timing for releasing the weapons into the hatch. Rose leaned over and glanced out the front view screen and then went back to the screens in front of her. Two seconds later her head whipped around and her face went sheet white.

"Uhm Emma, we are invisible on the alien's radar screens right?"

"Oh yes dear, but there is no worry about that because that is all that the aliens use to see into space."

"Oh right so that window above the ship's hatch that those aliens are looking out of and pointing at us, they really can't see us is what you are saying right?"

"Oh damn, hang on, my dears, weapons away," Emma said as the hatch opened and several fighters exited while a brace of six torpedoes went inside the ship.

"FIRE ALL LASERS, GIRLS!" Emma yelled as I felt the ship kick and we accelerated away from the command ship. Rose and I pushed the various laser firing switches as ships came within range on our radar screens and each of us let out yelps and screams as we felt the kicks from the return fire of the ships around us.

We were pulling away from the planet and the ships around us headed toward one of the small moons that circled this world. *"Hang on my dears we are going to whip around this little satellite and see if we can't lose some of these little pesky buggers."*

That was about when the space behind us lit up like another sun had been born and we were buffeted around even worse than before. "WHAT WAS THAT, EMMA?" Rose screamed.

"Oh that, my dear, was the command ship and most of the fighters and scout ships around it."

"How many more fighters are after us, Emma?" I asked as we started around the small moon.

"A few dear and as soon as we get a little ahead of them we will turn and wipe these little buggers off of us. When I give the order to,

sweeties, I want you to both hit all front lasers while I launch our front torpedoes, okay?"

"Yeah, sure, Emma, no problem," I said as I felt the ship flip around one hundred and eighty degrees so that we were now facing back the way we had come. About ten seconds later nearly twenty fighters from the command ship came screaming around the moon looking for blood.

"Now, dears, fire," Emma said as I felt the thumps of weapons leaving the front of the ship. A few ships, I thought, as I pressed down the fire triggers and watched as the fighters ran into a wall of death and destruction.

I could hear Rose next to me screaming as she pulled her own triggers and watched the ships turn into clouds of fire and dust. *"You can stop firing, dears, please, they are all gone."* Emma's voice slowly sank through my mind and I let up on the trigger as I heard Rose give a large sigh behind me.

I sat back in my chair and scanned the sky looking for any more fighters in the area. "Did we get them all, Emma," I asked.

"Yes, my dears I have scanned all the areas around the planet and can find no presence of aliens."

"Well, dears if it is still your plan to go to the alien home world there are a number of things that we will need to do first."

I looked over at Rose and she nodded back at me. "Yeah, Emma, we are still going to the alien home world and get those humans out of there."

"Then sweeties we need to first land back on the planet below and scrounge for any weapons, food and anything else we may need to save these humans. The second thing we need to do is for me to align my star maps since they are about one hundred and fifty years out of date or so."

"Well then lets head down to the planet and get what we need from our old home shall we," I said as I felt the ship flip once more and head down to our old home once again.

About an hour later, we landed outside of the main town on Ecstasy. On the way down, Emma warned us that a group of Tekis were on their way to the same area that we were aiming toward. "Come to loot what the aliens left behind?" I questioned Emma.

"Well, my dear, I am sure that the Teki did not fail to notice the rather large ship that was destroyed above them, so I am sure that they feel it only fair that they take whatever the aliens and humans left on this planet."

"How long do we have until the Teki get here, Emma?" Rose asked.

"By my estimates, you have two hours to collect all the various items we discussed that might be needed to rescue those on the alien home world."

"Okay, Emma, let's put down and get it over with," I said.

Emma landed about fifty feet from the north end of town. *"Alright dears the Teki are coming from the south, so I would like you to start at that end of town and gather all you can, that way you will be closer to me to make a quick getaway if you need to."*

Rose and I had our ear buds in, tuned to talk to Emma so that she would guide us to the stuff she thought we would need. As we stepped down from the ship, each of us carrying packs and the weapons we had used before on the alien ships, the rain came down in a light misty sheet that cut visibility down to ten feet or so.

"How we doing, Emma? Any life signs in town at all?" Rose asked in a hushed voice.

"No, my dears I will notify you as soon as I get any life signs close to you. Don't worry, I would never let anything happen to you two."

We started walking down the street toward the other end of town, with Rose taking one side of the street and I the other side. When we were halfway down I stopped and stared into the mist. "Rose, hold up. I see someone," I called quietly across the street.

Rose moved over next to me and looked down the side of the street I was looking at. "I don't see anything, Cassie."

I glanced over at my cousin and then back down the street where I could see two figures moving in the mist. "There, right there, can't you see them?" I said pointing with the tip of the small rifle in my hand.

"Emma do you have anything in front of us?" Rose

whispered into the mic that hung from the ear buds we wore.

"I'm sorry dears, but there are no life signs anywhere near you. The nearest Tekis are at least an hour and a half away still from this current position. I don't know what you are seeing, but there is no one here."

"Oh damn," I said as it registered what or who I was seeing down the street.

"Ghosts?" Rose said as we started walking once again.

"Yeah, ghosts," I answered as I looked around and saw that the mist was clearing up and that I could see more and more of the town's people wondering up and down the street. Many of them had this sort of lost surprised look on their face as they drifted past us.

"Who do you see, Cassie?" Rose asked, looking around seeing nothing but the empty town.

"All of them, Rose, I can see all the town people that lived here. The aliens must have killed everyone here after we took off."

"Are any of them talking to you, Cassie?"

"No, not so far, but they don't always talk to me, even if I can see them."

"Okay then let's get the stuff we came for then, Cassie, and get out of here," Rose said as she picked up the pace and started to run toward the outfitter's store down at the end of the street.

We finally got down to our first objective and found the doors locked. "Well with no one around I guess there is only one way to get what we need," Rose said as she stepped back and pointed her rifle at the front door.

"I wouldn't do that if I was you," a voice said to my right. I jumped, grabbing Rose's arm startling her as she pressed the trigger and the sidewalk in front of the doors suddenly had a large hole in it.

"Now look what you made me do, Cassie, settle down will you?"

"Sorry," I said as I looked to the right and saw a kid maybe a year older then Rose and I leaning up against the store wall.

"And why shouldn't we do that?" I asked the boy.

"Damn another ghost," I could hear Rose whisper next to me.

"I wouldn't do that because the alien's set traps in case someone came back here to get anything from the town, and if you shoot the doors open you will trip one of those traps," the boy said smiling as he continued to lean against the store wall.

I explained the problem to Rose as she turned pale at what could have been. "Okay, so do you know how we can get into the store without getting ourselves killed?"

"Oh, I think I may be able to do that for you for a price."

"Uhm what price and what is your name anyways?" I asked.

"My name is Billy and my price is that you take me with you."

"Uhm Billy you do know that you are dead and you can't leave the area you died at or are buried at. I don't understand how it works, but any ghost I've known has followed those rules," I said, feeling sorry for the boy standing in front of me as I told him the facts of life or death I guess you could say. I could see the smile slip off of his face at my news.

"You two are the ones that the aliens were looking for, aren't you?" Billy said now walking toward us and looking both of us over with some interest.

"Yeah, Billy, we are the ones, and I'm sorry that everyone got caught up in this. But the aliens would have wiped us all out no matter what. It is what they do."

"Yeah, I sort of guessed that, but you are sure that I'm dead and can't come with you?"

"Yeah, I'm sure, Billy, sorry about that."

"Uhm my dears why are you standing in front of the outfitters, you do know that you have a limited time to get all the stuff we need and

carry it back to me, right?"

"Yes, Emma, we know, it's just that Cassie is talking to a ghost and it seems that the aliens have set traps around town."

"Oh then you girls need to come back to the ship for the Teki are moving faster than I thought and will be in town in a little less than an hour, sweeties."

"Hold on a second, Emma," I said as I glanced over at Rose and then back toward Billy. "Listen Billy we need to get stuff out of town and down to our ship before the Teki come here. I'm sorry you are dead, but any help would be nice."

Billy stood there looking at us with a frown when Rose spoke up to the empty air where Billy stood. "Would it help if you knew that we killed the aliens that got you?"

Billy smiled at me even though Rose could not see the reaction that her words had had on the ghost that stood before us. "Well, in that case, girls, follow me."

We walked around the side of the building and up to the big doors in the side that were used for delivery of goods to the store. "The aliens laid traps on the front of the buildings, but not on the back or side doors."

"Okay so we can get in here," I said walking up to the door and seeing the combination lock. "Uhm I don't think we can blast our way in with this kind of lock, Billy?"

"Not a problem," he said as he walked up and tried to punch in a number to the lock. "Oh yeah, forgot I'm dead."

"Here let me do it. What is the number, Billy?" I said as I paused with my hand over the buttons on the lock.

"Oh yeah, it's 3345," Billy said as I punched in the number and Rose and I heard the lock click in the door.

"Alright Cassie, let's get these packs filled up with what we need."

As we pushed into the store, Billy followed us and watched us start to fill up our packs from the list that Emma had given us. "Uhm you know that there is a hover-trailer that will hold more stuff in it don't you?"

"Hold up, Rose," I said to my cousin and then turned back to Billy. "You have one of those here, Billy?"

"What, what did he want now?" Rose asked, looking around the store to see what was holding up our shopping trip now.

"Billy here says that there is a hover-trailer in the store we can use, Rose."

"Well, where is it?" Rose asked looking around the store for the trailer.

I looked at my cousin. "Well if you give me a second, I will find out."

"Sorry, Cassie."

"Okay, where is this trailer, Billy? Please? We are in a little hurry," I said looking at the ghost standing before me.

"Oh yeah, sure, no problem, it is right over here behind the counter," Billy said as he walked toward the front of the store with me following close behind.

When we got to the counter, sure enough, there was a state of the art hover-trailer used in town to move junk from one building to the next. Rose walked over and looked over the counter at our prize and then back up at me. "And you know how to use this how?"

I looked at Rose and then over at Billy. "Yeah, yeah, I can tell you how to use it," the ghost said with a sigh. "You know I wasn't ever this busy when I was alive."

"Okay then," I said hopping over the counter next to the trailer. "Rose, you go and find where everything is in this store while I get a quick lesson on trailer operations."

Folding Space

"Just to let you know, my dears, you have about fifteen minutes until the first of the Tekis enter the town, so please head back to me right now with what you have."

"Right Emma, we are on our way now," I said as Rose and I moved down the street with our horde of goodies that we had pillaged from the town. The hover-trailer that Billy had told me about had helped Rose and I carry a bigger load of stuff around town and saved us some shoe leather from walking back and forth from the various stores and Emma.

We got down the street in short order and had started loading the ship when we heard Emma's warning, *"Sweeties there are three Teki warriors entering the other end of town."*

"Damn! Now, what are we going to do, Cassie?"

"Ssh, I need to concentrate," I whispered as I let my mind open to see the innermost fears of the three Tekis walking into the town. Slowly I put together a picture of the creature that we had encountered in the last trek we had through the woods.

We both jumped in the air when we heard that weird wild cry and the yells of the Teki warriors. "Oh, you didn't Cassie!?!" Rose said as she looked down the street and turned white at the sounds that issued from that direction.

"Yeah, I did and I think it might be a good idea for us to finish up here and beat it before the Zeeky I conjured up gets tired of Teki and comes down here to get a taste of human."

"Uhm, dears, the three Teki individuals have been terminated by an animal life form. I am sorry that I did not detect this life form as it seemed to have popped up from thin air."

"Don't worry about it, Emma, I will explain how that animal came here sometime. We are almost done loading equipment so we should be ready to lift in a few minutes," I said as Rose and I had a quick laugh over Emma's surprise at the strange creature that showed up out of nowhere.

As I passed the last of the equipment up into the ship, we once more heard that weird cry of the creature in the woods behind us. "Uhm Cassie, how long do your manifestations usually last," Rose whispered

"Uhm not long, Rose, why do you ask?"

"Oh because it walked out of the woods behind you and it looks like it is still hungry."

"Oh," was all I could whisper as I slowly turned my head and looked over my shoulder. There crouched a large cat-like creature with six legs and two large fangs that extended from the top of the creature's mouth.

Its tail snapped back and forth above the backside, and its tufted ears pricked forward on the creature that looked like it would spring any second. "Emma," I whispered, "when you hear me say 'now' shut the door fast, please."

"I see your problem my dears, please wait a second."

"Wait for my butt," I said as I pushed Rose in the door and hopped up through it right behind her. I turned and watched the creature leaping through the air as a beam of light hit it dead center. There was a bright flash, a puff of smoke, and the smell of overdone bar-be-que where the creature had been only seconds ago.

"There was no need to hurry, hon, now please put away all this equipment while I take us back into space," Emma said as her door shut and we felt the gentle acceleration of the ship from this planet.

"Guess there was no need to hurry, Cassie," Rose said with a chuckle as she picked herself up off the deck of the ship and started to put equipment away in some storage holds that Emma had opened for us.

"Yeah, except it was my butt hanging out there for that creature's meal."

"That is true, Cassie, so maybe next time pull something

out of someone's mind that doesn't find you so tasty then."

"Yeah, no problem, cousin, I will try to remember that," I said as I got up and helped her pack away the supplies from our raid on the town.

After our quick departure from the only home we knew, Emma took us in orbit around one of the small moons of Ecstasy. After a quick visit each to the refresher cabinet, Rose and I were enjoying another hot meal that Emma had whipped up for us.

"Okay, Emma now why are we sitting here enjoying the view of the stars?" I asked between mouthfuls of the food I was chowing down on.

"Well my dear, if you want to end up in the middle of a sun or another planet we can take off any old time you want. Since I have been down on that planet for over one hundred and fifty years in the main ship and under cloud cover, I figured it would be a good idea to update my charts."

Both Rose and I gulped down the food we had been chewing and looked at each other. "Yeah, that's okay Emma don't mind Cassie she is a little cranky from almost being cat chow," Rose said as she smiled at me and winked to take the sting out of her comment.

"Oh yeah, Emma, I never did like cats especially when they

wanted to make me into a chew toy. So how long do you think it will take until we have good charts?"

"Oh, sweeties I think that I will have the charts figured out within the hour."

"Oh, that won't be too bad then we can head out toward the alien's home world?" I asked the ship.

"Well first, my dears, what I would like to do is to make a short hop to test the updated charts."

"Okay, where do you want to hop to Emma?"

"Well, hon, I thought we would first try to hop to where our original flight started from."

Rose and I once more glanced at each other as the same thought crossed our minds. "Uhm Emma didn't the Captain rescue the people from that planet because the aliens were there and taking over?" I asked.

"You are right dear, but I want to go there for two reasons."

"And those are?"

"The first is that it will be a small jump in comparison to jumping to the alien's home world, so we will know if my charts are accurate or if they are out of balance."

"And you want a small jump because?" Rose asked.

"Oh that is simple, my dear, the smaller the jump the smaller the error if my charts are out of balance."

"Okay makes sense, and then what is the second reason for this small jump of yours."

"Well, my dears I want to see if the aliens have taken over the planet like we think they did. That way when we rescue the humans on the alien home world and get back to Earth, we can give them some idea of what is out there waiting for them."

"Uhm Emma, it's one planet; what can the Earth people learn from that?"

"Well actually sweeties, I thought we could maybe, just perhaps, take small hops throughout the systems until we get to the alien's homeworld. In that way, we can check out each planet that humans were on, and it is mostly on a direct course to our destination."

Rose looked over at me and shrugged her shoulders like she didn't care about the slight shift in plans, and looking at it the way Emma presented it, it wasn't all that bad of an idea. Plus it is hard to say no to a ship that pleaded in that tone of voice. "Okay, Emma we do it your way, as soon as you update your charts."

"Thank you, my dears, you are such nice girls," Emma said.

Yeah, nice pushovers is what she meant, though. I stood up and collected the plate from Rose and started to head back toward the galley to clean up when Emma spoke again, *"Oh and sweeties I will have my charts done in one half hour, so please walk the inside and make sure that all items are secured for when we do the jump."*

"Sure Emma," Rose said as she got up and started to clean

up around the control room. I looked around and saw that the control room looked a lot like my room back home after a weekend slumber party that Rose and I had had when we were younger.

"Sorry, Emma, for the mess, we'll try to keep you cleaner from now on."

"Oh no problem dear, it's nice actually to have someone living inside me once again. It was so boring to sit there for that long without any company you know. I was so lonely until you girls came along."

"Uhm Emma if it was so easy to leave like you did when we came along, how come you stayed there all this time?"

"Oh, why sweeties heaven forbid if I left the Captain or the Commander stranded on that planet. Why I could never do that."

"Okay Emma, but didn't you think that after that long of a time that the two of them weren't around anymore?" I asked.

There was a slight hesitation before Emma spoke again. *"Well yes dear, but you see after a little while I sort of shut down all my external sensors and kind of hibernated. Every so often I would send out a low signal to my sister, but, of course, she never answered me, and of course with that damn cloud cover always over the planet I could never get a clear look at the stars, and well. . ."*

"Yeah, no problem Emma, don't sweat the small stuff. I would probably do the same thing as you if I was all alone by myself," Rose said.

"Yeah, me too, Emma."

"Oh well thank you, dears. Like I said before, you are the best company a girl like me could hope for."

Both Rose and I glanced at each other and then up at the speaker as the laughter erupted from the two of us.

"Alright, sweeties what is so funny?" Emma asked, a hurt tone coming from the speakers overhead.

"Oh, we aren't laughing at you, Emma, as much as that we are laughing with you, okay?" I asked.

"Okay dears, I guess I will never understand you, silly girls. My charts are now up to date, my dears, so please finish cleaning up and take your seats in the control room."

So Rose and I finished our clean up chores and hit the control room to settle in for the first mini jump. As we sat down and started to buckle up, I could feel the seats start to slide back into an incline position.

"Uhm Emma, what's up with the seats?" I asked looking over to see that my cousin was now in the same supine position as I was.

"No fear, dears, it is just that when we fold space it was found that the human body tolerated the flight better in this position," Emma said as a metal cover slid down over the front view screen.

"Uhm we aren't going to fold space by Ecstasy, Emma, are we? I mean I have no gripe against the people on this planet."

"No dear, I have taken us beyond the last planet of the system and we will be making the first jump in a few minutes."

"Oh okay Emma, I was just. . ." my words were cut off in mid-sentence as the area in front of me started to waver back and forth and suddenly the front of the ship stretched out to eternity. I tried to turn my head to look at Rose as I heard a strangled cry from her direction, but it felt like my head weighed a million pounds and it was locked down into its current position. Then it I felt a sharp prick in my arm and all went black.

"Please wake up, my dears," I heard a concerned voice whisper.

"Five more minutes, mommy," I heard Rose mumble across from me.

"Come on, sweeties, time to rise and shine – up and at 'em," the voice was louder now or maybe my hearing was coming back.

I opened my eyes and found myself staring out at a star field in front of the window. "Emma is that you?" I whispered because talking any louder would intensify the killer headache that was pounding in my head and driving down my spine.

"Yes, dear, it is me. Can you check your cousin, because I don't think she is fully awake yet?"

"Yeah, no problem. Give me a second, I feel like my head is going to split in two."

"I am sorry, dear, but that may have been the drug that I gave you when we made the jump."

I sat there not saying a word while I slowly counted to one hundred in my head.

"Cassie my dear, are you mad at me again?" Emma whispered.

I took in a breath of air and then slowly let it out as I centered my anger and then let it wash out of me. "No Emma, I'm not mad," I said as I turned toward the low moan that issued from beside me. I looked over at Rose and saw her bent over in her seat, her head held in her hands.

"Rose, are you okay?" I whispered while I moved gradually out of my seat and kneeled next to my cousin.

"I will be, Cassie, as soon as the two of you stop shouting," Rose whispered back and then once more moaned into her hands.

"Here drink this, dears," Emma said as two glasses of a bubbling concoction slid out of a door on the front control panel.

"Oh, will it kill me? Please tell me it will, Emma," Rose

whispered as she looked at the two glasses while sniffing the vapor that floated up from the bubbling liquid.

"WHAT!?! Why of course not, sweeties, why would you even think I would do something that bad to you?"

"Oh, I was hoping that it would, Emma, with the way I feel," Rose whispered as she took her glass from me and downed the foul-smelling liquid as I did mine. My head was pounding even more than before as if that was possible since I had moved from my chair to help my cousin.

After downing the drink in hand, Rose sat back in her chair with her eyes shut while I slowly sank down to the floor of the ship. The liquid hit my stomach like a small bomb and then I felt the warmth spread outward throughout my body. As it hit my limbs and it moved up my spine, I could feel the pounding in my head dissipate while the room slowly stopped spinning.

"Uhm Emma, are we going to have to go through this each jump we make?" I said in a whisper, still not taking any chances that a loud noise would bring back the pounding in my head.

"No, my dears, for some reason the only time you will have a problem is the first jump. After that, the body gets used to the jump and you will not have any more troubles. At least that is the theory my maker had about it."

"Uhm Emma, I thought you said that you had been doing trial flights and were ready for your maiden voyage."

"Well see that is true in a sense, but we had never really tried a jump before with humans on board before today, but right now there is another small problem that we have, girls."

"You know Emma, I think one day we really need to sit down and hash out exactly what you have done and can do and talk about telling us the whole truth, and not what you think we need to know."

"Well yes that is fine, dear, but there is still the little problem we seem to have."

"NO, no more other problems, Emma. We need to figure out some things here and nothing is more important than that right now."

"Well okay, hon, then you don't want me to tell you about the other aliens that are now on the planet below us?"

Bugs!

In the quiet that followed her announcement, the only sound you could hear in the control room was the light hiss of air coming from the vents above us. "Emma is that 'other alien' you're talking about a wholly different type from the ones we knew about?" Rose whispered in the quiet.

"Yes, dears I'm afraid that is exactly what I mean."

"Okay, Emma forget about what I said before and spill everything you know about these other aliens and where they came from," I said getting up from the floor and slumping back into my chair.

"Alright, dears, I will. First, the aliens that we know about from their computer records are called the Mordunes. These people live on a home world that is nine/tenths water. They live along coasts of any land and mine and farm the water around them. In fact, I don't see why they and humans would run into conflicts at all because both species could equally share a planet – Humans on land and the Mordunes in the water."

"Uhm okay Emma then who or what are these other creatures and why are they on a planet that the Mordunes were supposed to have taken from us one hundred and fifty years ago?" I asked.

"Well from what I can gather from scans of this planet, the Mordune's cities around the coast have all been destroyed and the rest of the planet has been divided up into mining and farming sites by these new aliens."

"And what of the human cities that were on this planet, Emma?"

"Basically, my dears those have been wiped off the face of the planet, and replaced by the before mentioned sites of mining and farming."

"How about spaceships and such, Emma?" Rose asked.

"There is some debris floating around the planet from Human and Mordune ships, along with three ships that I must assume is of the new alien's design as they fit neither of the other specs in the Human or Mordune's computers."

"Emma, can we get close enough to check out what these aliens look like?"

"Yes, dears I am working on that now. We will soon be on the other side of the planet from the alien ships and over one of the smaller farm areas on this side."

"Can they see us, Emma?" Rose asked with some concern in her voice.

"As far as I can tell, hon, they haven't spotted us. I figured if we were going to get a closer view of these aliens it might be a good idea to have a planet between us and their ships, just in case."

"Good thinking, Emma. How long before we get into contact range?"

"We are settling into orbit now, dears. I have views on your screens of the aliens," Emma said as pictures appeared on a screen in front of me.

Rose came over and looked over my shoulder at the pictures of the aliens on this planet. The picture showed a view of a planted field with some of the aliens working between the borders of the field. "What are they?" Rose asked of the strange creatures we could see working.

"My dears, these people are similar to what on old Earth was called an ant," Emma said as a picture of a creature appeared next to the view screen we were looking at. Sure enough looking at the three segmented body of the Earth ant we could see the resemblance to the aliens on this world.

Looking at the picture of the Earth insect and the alien, I noticed a few differences such as the aliens seemed to have arms and movable digits where the ant's front legs were. Also, it appeared that these creatures were a whole lot bigger than any ant according to the information on the view screen that Emma had provided for us.

"Dears, there is one thing you should know."

"What's that, Emma?" I asked.

"Well, it seems that there are no communication signals down on the planet or around the ships in orbit."

"Okay, then how do they communicate, Emma?"

"I don't have enough information to make a guess, my dears, but however they do it it is not the same way that Humans or Mordunes do."

"Okay, Emma so we now have a second alien race to deal with, what do you recommend that we do?"

"My dears, I think that we make another jump to the next planet in the outer rim and see what we find there."

I sat there for a second and then looked at Rose who had turned a little white at Emma's plan. "Okay, Emma let's make the jump."

Rose and I buckled up into our seats and felt them once again lean back in anticipation for the jump. As before I felt a strange sensation and the lights flickered and then the ship settled down to its normal shape and appearance.

"Uhm Emma, are we there yet?" Rose whispered.

"No dear, we will arrive in one hour ship time."

"Okay, this doesn't seem as bad as it did last time, Emma."

"As I said before, sweeties, each jump the Human body adjusts to the sensations created by folding space."

"Uhm can we see how folded space looks, Emma?" I

asked, curiosity burning to see what folding space would look like.

"That would not be wise, hon, for you see it was found that your Human minds could not handle the concept of what is happening around the ship and space while jumping. In fact, in testing the Human subjects all went mad."

"Okay then don't worry about it, Emma, I don't need to see what it looks like after all," I said and then yawned and stretched out the best I could strapped into my chair.

"What I would suggest, my dears, is that you each get a quick nap in. I thought that maybe you would like to see about going down to the next planet, if possible, to explore these new aliens."

"Yeah, not a bad idea, Emma," I said as I looked over at Rose and could see that her eyes were already closed. I shifted around in my chair the best I could and then slowly let the quiet of the control room seep over my body, letting my eyes close as the lights dimmed and soft music started to play.

"Wake up dears," the quiet voice sounded from above. *"We are here and I have moved us within orbit for the next planet."*

"Thanks, Emma," I said as the seat rose to an upward position and I unbuckled the belts that strapped me into it.

"How does this planet look, Emma?" Rose asked.

"I am sorry to say that this planet, like the other one, is inhabited by this second alien race. As before I can detect no radio transmissions from the ground and from the two ships that orbit this world."

"Okay how about us going down to explore and find out a little more about these aliens?"

"I have found a small area that seems to be sitting bare with no crops planted with few aliens around for now. If we land there, you could try to get into the buildings in the area and I will see if we can't hook into whatever computer system they may have."

I looked over at Rose and she nodded at me in agreement with the plan we had conjured up before. "Okay Emma, take us down and let's see if we can't figure something out about these creatures," I said as Rose and I got up and headed back to the airlock and the weapons locker.

Thirty minutes later, we were down on the planet hidden in a small valley just beyond our target point. Rose and I were both tired from climbing one of the small hills that lined the valley. I was really getting to love space travel, but it seemed to play hell on your conditioning.

As we topped the hill, I looked back and saw that beyond the valley and the hills behind it I could see the sea. It seemed like the valley was a catch-all in case the water out there breached the first wall instead of some natural formation.

Looking around at the dark areas around us, I could see all

the land spread out in the bright moonlight. Below us, I could spy some buildings with pipes coming out of the ground near them and what looked like unplanted fields stretching as far as the eye could see.

"Well, what do you think, Emma?" I asked after I told her what lay below us.

"I think you two dears need to be very careful when you go down to the building below. I detect life forms, but they are well below the surface of this planet."

"Didn't the information you gave us on Earth ants say something about them living underground, Emma?" Rose asked.

"Yes sweeties, but remember that these are aliens and not of Earth so that there may be a lot of differences that we don't know about."

"We'll keep that in mind, Emma," I said as I started down the hill with Rose in tow. About halfway down I found a trail that led down the hill toward the buildings below which made it simpler to walk down.

As we got closer to the bottom of the hill I could see the land around us better and saw that the unplanted area around us wasn't quite as bare as I thought at the top of the hill. Looking around, I could see small plants poking up through the ground. "Uhm Emma this area isn't unplanted after all. It looks like we have some new shoots coming up through the ground."

"That is not good, dears, how about you come back to the ship and we

forget this whole thing? I am sure that we can find some other way to find out more about these creatures."

By this time, we had made it to where we were almost behind the building with the pipes coming out of it. Rose and I both stopped and were resting for a second before we went any further when I looked over at her. Rose shook her head and pointed toward the buildings with a smile.

"No that's alright, Emma, I think we need to stick to the original plan," I said.

"Then I think I need to come get you, dears, for your own good."

"EMMA," I said in a harsh whisper, "stay where you are, we will let you know if we need help. Do not come unless we call."

"Yes hon, but I have an oh so bad feeling about this."

Rose and I ignored our over-protective friend, ship, mother figure or whatever she thought she was and headed down the last bit of hill to the back end of the building below us. Leaning up against the building, we stood there listening to the sounds of the night.

After a couple of minutes of standing there in the night listening to the buzzing sounds of unfamiliar insects and small flying creatures that flew past us, we moved slowly around the building until we came to a large door. "Think it's locked?" Rose asked.

"I guess there is only one way to find out, isn't there?" I

said as I reached down and pushed on the door, opening it into the dark room that hid behind it. We both stood there, me holding the door open as far as it would go letting the bright moonlight shine inside the room giving up its shadowed secrets.

I looked around for something to hold the door open when Rose handed me a small wedge shaped rock from the ground. "Thanks," I whispered as I jammed the rock under the door hoping that it would hold it open so that it would give us enough light to see by without using the lights we had brought with us from the ship.

Moving inside, I could see that we were in a control room with dials, wheels, several tubes of water, and pipes everywhere you looked. *"Have you dears seen any computer terminals anywhere,"* Emma whispered into our ears.

"Yeah, over here, Cassie," Rose said as she moved over to a bank of machines, taking the computer drive out of her pocket and plugging it into a hole in the console.

"Ahhh yes that is a good girl, you found it on the first try. Now this will take a few minutes as it did on the Mordune's ship."

While we were waiting for Emma to do her thing, Rose and I decided to do a little exploring. I was looking at the glass tubes that were around the room and noticed that they all were attached to the pipes that ran along the ceiling and out the sides of the buildings. Looking at them I noticed that each tube had a stopper that you could push to get a drop of liquid out of them.

"Cassie? What are you doing?" Rose asked as I pushed up one of the stoppers and a small drop of liquid leaked out onto my finger.

"Salt water from the sea, I think," I said as I touched the liquid to my tongue.

"Uhm you know that isn't very smart, Cassie. What if that was some poison or something."

I blanched at that thought but knew it didn't matter anymore. "Sorry cousin," I said as I wiped the rest of the liquid off on my pants.

"Uhm sweeties, you need to leave that building right now."

"What's wrong, Emma? Are you done getting the information you need?" I asked.

"No, dears, I haven't, but. . ."

"No, we're staying until you get what you need, Emma. We can wait a few minutes more," Rose whispered.

"No, dears, you can't wait anymore for I detect movement from a small body of aliens that are now moving from below ground to your position. Now move please and I will come and pick you up."

Rose and I froze in place for a second and then I could hear a sound like the sweeping of dry branches against the house coming from a dark opening across the room. "How many are coming, Emma, and how long for you to finish downloading what you need?" I asked pointing my weapon at the dark opening as the sound continued to get louder by the second.

"It does not matter, hon, you need to leave now dears."

"Emma, answer me! How long to finish the download?"

"Five more minutes dears, but please leave now," Emma said as her voice took on that pleading tone that my momma had used when she really wanted me to do something she thought was important.

"Yeah, not until you're done downloading, Emma," I said, moving over to the console and putting my hand over the computer drive ready to pull it out and head to the door as soon as Emma gave me the okay.

"OH DAMN, Cassie look." I heard Rose say as she pointed her weapon at the dark opening that now held one of the aliens we had seen on Emma's view screen while in orbit. I can tell you now that close up these guys looked a whole lot scarier than they did from space.

The creature that filled the opening looked around the room, its antennas waving in the air as though searching for some vibe or sound from us. It turned its large egg-shaped head toward Rose as she yelled out to me and took a step toward her, those big round eyes zeroing in on my cousin.

Before it could take another step, we both let loose some shots with our weapons that hit the creature dead center in its creepy face. The good thing for us was that as large as the creature was, it was hard to miss it. The bad thing was that the creature stumbled back a few feet and then shook its head and started back toward my cousin. Oh, this was so not good, I thought, especially since I could see another creature coming up from behind the first one.

"SHOOT ITS LEGS" Rose yelled as two bright blasts from her weapon hit the creature's two middle right legs. This seemed to be having a better effect as I saw the creature's legs buckle and it go down sideways, but it still kept trying to come forward, and the creatures behind it started to push it forward and out of their way.

"Dears, shoot the white pipes above you," I could hear Emma say over the discharge of our rifles.

"UHM EMMA WE ARE A LITTLE BUSY NOW, TELL US WHEN THE DOWNLOAD IS DONE, AND COME GET US," I yelled at the ship not really in the mood for any games right now.

"The download is done, I am outside waiting, now shoot the white pipes because they are filled with salt water and that is like acid to these creatures. DO IT NOW AND RUN!"

By the time that Emma had finished her scolding, I had pulled the computer drive from the console and was backing toward the door in the deluge of saltwater that was raining down on us from the pipes that we had both blasted to bits.

Sure enough, like Emma said, as soon as the water hit the skin of the creatures we could see it peel and slough off of their bodies, not the prettiest sight I can tell you. The creatures that had been moving up behind the first few though were still trying their hardest to come at us even through the waterfall of saltwater that was coming down from the ceiling. Their actions and that they made no sound at all while they were literally melted by the water seemed to spur us both out the door in a hurry and over to the open hatch of our ship.

Before we hit the ship's hatch, I saw a bright streak pass over our heads from one of Emma's blasters and glanced over my shoulder and watched as the outside pipes peeled back and salt water shot up into the sky drenching us even more than before. *"Okay, dears, that should keep them busy for awhile so hop into the ship and let's get out of here."*

As my butt cleared the hatch, I felt it shut and then I felt a sudden acceleration of the ship which threw me into my cousin. "What the hel. . ."

"Sorry, dears, had to take us out of orbit and out of reach of the alien's ships coming around the planet."

"Uhm, no problem, Emma. By the way, thanks for the save back there," I said picking myself up off of my cousin and then giving her a hand up from the floor. "Are we safe now?"

"Yes, sweeties, you are safe now. We are hiding behind the third planet in this system, and there are no more aliens to worry about anyways."

"Emma, what did you do?" Rose asked.

"Well, dears when I took us to our position I sort of folded a little bitty space and well there is now no more planet or alien ships."

Rose and I stared at each other as we put our equipment away and then we both turned without saying a word and marched back toward the ship's control room.

Rescue

"Now sweeties, before you say anything, let me explain," Emma said as we both arrived in the control room and marched over to the main console.

"Okay Emma, explain what exactly?"

"You see, dears, I got some information from my download that made it imperative to you that I destroy these aliens."

"Okay, we're listening, Emma. What's the information that you got?"

"Well see, sweeties, these aliens are not only farmers, but they are herders also," Emma whispered.

"Okay so they herd animals, so what? We humans do that too for food," I stated.

"Yes I know, dears, but according to their records these aliens consider the Humans and Mordunes on the same level that you would your own herd animals."

"What? Are you telling us that we are something like food

to them?" I asked.

"If we're herd animals to them, how do they explain that we have space travel," Rose said.

"I'm sorry, dears, but it seems that these aliens do not look at any other creature as having the intelligence that they have."

"Okay, so what other good news can you tell us about these aliens, Emma?"

"I can tell you, hon, that these creatures are the main reason that you and the Mordunes are at war."

"Really and how did they accomplish that little feat, Emma?"

"It seems that the Captain and the Commander were wrong on one point. The Mordunes were on this planet before Humans, but it was this alien race that wiped out the first attempt by them to settle the planet. When Humans came to the planet to settle the Mordunes thought that the Humans had taken the planet from them so they wiped them out. They, in turn, were, for the most part, wiped out by these new aliens except for the few that were kept as food, that is."

"Okay, that is a creepy thought," I whispered to no one in particular.

"Well, I guess I can't get mad at you for getting rid of them then, Emma. Last thing I wanted to be today was dinner for some ant. Thanks again for coming back and for saving our butts," Rose stated.

"No problem, sweeties, it is always a privilege to keep you two alive and kicking."

"Okay, what do we do now that we know about these creatures?" I asked.

"Well from what I understand from the alien computer, I would think that the best thing to do would be to get the Humans that are on the Mordune's home world and head back to Earth as soon as possible."

"Okay, Emma what are you hiding that we should know?" I questioned the ship.

"Well dears, according to the computer, the next target for these aliens is the Mordune's home world. Since that world is ninth/tenths salt water the planet has no interest to these aliens as a settlement so they are not out to take over the world but to destroy it totally and all creatures on it."

Rose and I stared at each other, each thinking her own thoughts on how this mess we had got ourselves into seemed to be getting bigger and bigger every time we turned around. "Okay, Emma let's see if we can't go save some Humans," I said as Rose and I climbed into each of our chairs and started to buckle ourselves into them for the next jump.

With the long jump that we had ahead of us, Emma recommended that we be given some drugs to help us sleep during the trip. Neither one of us was keen on going through the experience that we had on our first jump, but Emma promised us that wouldn't happen on this time around.

We buckled in after Emma urged us to use the refresher cabinet and grab some food before we did our jump. After eating and getting clean, we were ready once more for the next trip in our adventure.

"You know, Emma, I really hate needles — did you know that?" I said as I watched a small syringe pop out of the console in front of me.

"I am sorry, hon, but I promise that you will be in better shape if you sleep through the trip we need to make."

"How long will this jump be again, Emma?" Rose asked.

"This will be a three-day trip, dears. When you wake it will take a little while for you to gain your energy and such back, but I promise you this is for the best as I said before."

"Fine let's get this done and over with Emma," I groused at the ship.

I felt a tiny prick in my arm as I heard Emma's whisper come from above us, *"Sweet sleep, dears, see you in three days,"* as the darkness of the drugs took me down into a long slumber.

"Alright sweeties, time to wake up," Emma's whispered voice floated down from above.

I felt the seat slowly move into an upright position and I stretched my aching muscles as much as I could in the confines of the chair's buckles. "What went wrong, Emma? Why did you wake us so soon?"

"It has been three days, hon, and we are just outside the Mordune's home system," Emma said as the odor of two bodies that had lain in sleep for three days assaulted my nose.

"Oh damn, one of us needs to visit the refresher cabinet," Rose said with a laugh and quick glance in my direction.

"Oh, cousin you don't smell like a summer flower yourself there," I answered with my own laugh.

"I would suggest, dears, that one of you goes to the refresher and the other go get the meal that I have provided you," Emma said once more in that motherly tone that she seemed to have picked up somewhere in our travels.

"Alright, stinkiest one to the refresher," both my cousin and I said at the same time as we both bolted out of our chairs toward the aroma of hot food that was traveling down the passageway of the ship.

"Fine girls, eat first then the refresher cabinet," both of us heard as we stumbled down the passageway, our laughter following us and drowning out Emma's slight rebuke.

After wolfing down some of Emma's hot food – it's

surprising how you can gain an appetite after three days of sleeping – and some time in the refresher, Rose and I were ready for anything that Emma could throw at us, or at least I thought we were.

"Now, dears, that we are all ready to go here I have a couple of tidbits for you."

"Okay shoot, Emma, what's up?" Rose asked as she stretched out on the floor of the ship and arched her back like a cat after a long sleep.

"Well, first there is the little problem of that pesky new alien race that has entered this system and is now headed toward the same planet that we are."

"Damn," I cussed and then looked up at the speaker above me. "Sorry Emma, but how long until they get to the planet and can we get there first?"

"Oh please, hon, of course, we will get there first by two days, but the aliens have no intention of taking this planet, only of destroying it so whatever we need to do to rescue the humans we will need to do it fast."

"Well alright then, we need to move fast so let's get on with it, Emma," I said as Rose got up off the floor and sat down in her chair and started, like me, to buckle herself in.

"Well see my dears there is the slight, little, itty, bitty other problem."

"And that problem is what, Emma? All I can see is you wasting time," I snapped back at her.

"Well, hon, the problem seems to be that the Mordune's computer was either wrong or not updated because after scanning the surface, I now come up with five hundred Humans on the Mordune's home world."

Rose and I glanced at each other and then out at the stars outside the ship. "Well, I guess we get as many out as we can, Emma," I said.

"Okay, dears, if you say so. It can be done at night I guess since from my scans all Humans are put together in one place. Of course, there is one other thing, that isn't really a problem per se as that it is something that you may want to know about."

"Okay, spill Emma," I said really getting tired of her games by now.

"Well remember those two life forms that I said were on the main ship and then were terminated?"

"Yeah, those life forms that were my parents, Emma, what about them?" I asked.

"Well you see, dear, it seems that those two life forms are now among the Humans on the Mordune's home world."

Once again there was silence in the control room so that only the sound of the air coming from the vents was heard. "Emma are you telling me that my parents are alive and down on that planet, is that what you are telling me?"

"Uhm yes?"

"But how?" I asked Emma.

"Well it seems from what I can tell that the aliens on the Command ship sent your parents to their home world on a special fast scout ship, I somehow missed it in the middle of all our actions that day."

"Then what are we waiting here for? Let's get down to the planet and get them out of there," I said.

"Alright, my dears, I wanted you to know all the facts before we headed down to the planet." With those words, Rose and I felt a kick in our chairs and we soon saw through the view screen that we were now closing in on the planet below us.

The night sky was black. Black and cold with the stars showing in the dark sky, and a bitter wind blowing across the flat plains that housed the landing field before us. We had landed last night after some tricky flying by Emma to avoid being seen by anyone on the ground. After being on the ground for a day, Emma was able to remotely hook into the planet's computer system and assured us that the Mordunes were now more interested in the approaching aliens than in us.

Across from where we were lying, we could see various ships being readied for launch. Most of them were ships of war with transports, and cargo ships mixed in. Rose and I lay on some rocks at the edge of the field, watching the one ship that we were hoping we could liberate from its owners.

"I don't know, Cassie, it doesn't look like it can get off the ground let alone take us back to Earth," Rose whispered, looking at the old transport that was our target for tonight.

"It's not like we have much choice in the matter, it's this one with the smallest crew or one of the warships," I said, not entirely disagreeing with her assessment of the ship before us.

"Are you dears ready for the action to begin?" Emma whispered into the ear buds we each wore.

"Yeah, Emma let the fireworks begin," I said loosening the strap on the rifle I held and getting ready to run to the transport and take command of it.

"But, dear, I'm not going to shoot fireworks at the Mordunes, for I don't think that that will do much good in our present circum. . ."

"Emma, please get going and shoot whatever you are going to shoot," I whispered trying hard to keep the annoyance I felt out of my voice as I heard Rose trying to stifle a giggle next to me. I looked over at Rose and whispered in her general direction, "You know you are only encouraging her, right?"

Rose ducked her head and looked at the ground and I heard a mutter of 'sorry' from my cousin. About two minutes later, I felt rather than saw or heard Emma settle above the middle of the flight line full of ships. As bolts of energy flashed from her sides and torpedoes flew up in the air and came down on top of ships, Rose and I bolted from our hiding place and headed toward the transport that I hoped would fit our needs.

Both of us hit the gangway and were through the open hatch before any of the aliens knew we were there. Two quick shots from each of us took care of the four aliens that had been crowding the airlock. "You take care of these guys and I'll see if there are any more problems on this ship," I said to Rose as I moved down the only passageway that hopefully led to the control room.

"Okay, watch your back," Rose said as the shooting outside stopped but the explosions from the ships that were hit kept the night loud and brightly lit. I really needed to find that control room and get us out of here fast. Emma was going to make sure that she didn't hit any ships in our area, but as she said before when you mix lasers, torpedoes, and fueled ships one never knew what was going to go boom in the dark.

I found the control room with no other encounters and plugged the computer drive that Emma gave us into the console before me. "Rose, got rid of those bodies yet?"

"Yeah, they are gone and the lock is secure, Cassie."

"Okay, thanks. Get up to the control room then. Emma, we are ready here. The drive is in the console and ready to go," I said buckling into the chair I had thrown myself into.

"That is fine, hon, I have a connection and I'm downloading the flight instructions now, give me one minute."

One minute sure no problem, I thought, as I felt the ship we were in rock from a nearby explosion. "I don't think we may have one minute, Emma," I said as Rose came up to the control room and threw herself into the nearest chair and proceeded to buckle up.

"Okay, my dears, here we go," Emma said as we both felt the engines kick in and the ship lifted off the ground and turned toward the direction of the camp where the rest of Humanity was waiting.

As we approached the camp, we both watched once more as Emma came down right in the middle of the buildings as she had done to the ships on the flight line. Emma had told us on the way to the camp that there were no guards there as everyone on this planet was more interested in getting off of it then guarding some left over Humans.

Of course, there still were some automatic weapon systems that were still operating in the camp, but as we watched from the transport Emma made short work of those with more torpedoes and laser fire.

"Alright my dears the way is clear now, get as many of these people out of here as you can," Emma said as she rose out of the way and the transport we were riding landed in the middle of the camp.

We both threw ourselves out of our chairs and rushed toward the hatch and the people we could see waiting below on the view screen. "Emma, how much time do we have?" I asked hitting the latch to open the doors before us.

"We have eight hours until the aliens are in range of this planet, but I think the Mordunes are getting wise to what is happening here so the sooner we go, the better."

"Okay got you, Emma, we will move as fast. . ." I started to say when I heard a voice I never thought I would hear again.

"Cassie? Rose? Is that you?" the voice of my momma sounded from the dark before us.

"MOMMA!" I yelled as I ran toward the figure now coming into the light from the ship. I thought that with some five hundred people, it would take awhile for me to find my parents and here I get off the ship and walk into my momma's arms.

"Damn, Cassie I thought we would never see you again. How did you get here?" I heard the gruff voice of my daddy ask from behind my momma and then I was pulled into his strong arms and hugged until I couldn't breathe.

"Uhm guys, Cassie, remember aliens coming to destroy the planet, need to go now," Rose said from behind me.

My momma looked at me and then Rose and stepped over to my cousin and enveloped her into the same huge hug that she had given me a few seconds ago. Rose forgot all about aliens and such as I had. I watched her sink her head into momma's shoulder and hugged back just as tight as she was given.

I could hear a few quiet sobs come from my cousin and a low whisper from my momma comforting her, but I knew she had been right – we didn't have a whole lot of time for a family reunion.

"Listen, daddy and momma, we need to get people on this ship and get out of here now," I said as I stepped out of my daddy's embrace and looked at the people that were gathering around us.

"Why? What is going on, Cassie? Who is in that other ship?" my daddy questioned as he looked up into the night sky looking for Emma.

"We really don't have time to tell you all of our adventures right now. Let's say that if we don't get off this planet now it won't be here for long," I said.

"Dears, I have finished checking out the ship's computer. It is a special transport that will hold all the Humans that are here. It was built for, hold on. . ." Two streaks of light flashed from the front of Emma and there was an explosion off in the distance. *"This ship, my dears, was built with sleep chambers and they will work for humans,"* Emma said into Rose and my ear buds.

"What was that explosion, Emma?" I asked.

"You need to get everyone onboard now, hon. The Mordunes, for some reason, are a little angry at us stealing this ship. Seems like they had plans of their own for this transport, now move these people on it and fast while I keep the Mordunes away."

"Alright listen to me, everyone," I said to the crowd gathered around us. "There are aliens coming to destroy this planet so if you want to get off of it, we need to load everyone on this transport and get out of here, like yesterday."

Everyone, including my parents, stood there for a minute and looked at me as if I had grown a second head that is until Rose raised her weapon in the air and fired off a shot and yelled, "COME ON, PEOPLE; YOU HEARD HER – MOVE IT NOW!"

Everyone ducked down for a second and then they all moved out gathering the ones that were still in the buildings and the surrounding area and headed toward the transport. Rose and I grabbed my parents and headed up the ramp of the ship while giving them a very quick and dirty run down of what was going on out in the wild universe around us.

As the people came up to the ship, with Emma's help, we got them settled down into the transport's hold for takeoff. After two hours of loading and twice Emma having to destroy several Mordune's fighters coming close to the camp, we were finally ready to go.

"Alright, my dears I have programmed this ship to take you to Earth."

"Uhm Emma you need to land so that Rose and I can come aboard," I said.

"Sorry, no time for that dear when we get out of this system we will need to get the people into the sleep chambers as the trip back to Earth will take a year in that ship," Emma said as the hatch of the transport shut and the engines started up.

As we launched into space once again a few more Mordunes came up to play, but Emma swatted them out of the night sky as though they were flies. We were soon headed out of the Mordune's home system and pointed toward Earth, a small gathering of what was left of humanity in this part of the system.

Finding Earth

"Wake up dears, you really need to wake up now, something is very wrong," Emma whispered in my ear as the top of the sleep chamber opened.

I slowly sat up and looked across the control room at the other sleep chambers and saw that only Rose was up and semi-awake like I was. "What's up, Emma? Are we there yet?" My voice croaked, feeling like sandpaper was lining the inside of my throat.

"Yes, my dears, we are near Earth or at least I am. Your ship is hiding behind the moon of Earth for right now."

"Okay, so what's the problem, Emma?" Rose whispered, apparently her throat in no better condition than mine.

"Well, sweeties, it seems that the aliens that were out to take over the Mordunes have done the same to Earth."

"Uhm damn, you mean they beat us here, the aliens I

mean?"

"No, dears, the aliens that were destroying the Mordune's home world will not be going anywhere nor doing what they did to anyone else," Emma said with an evil chuckle.

"Do we want to know what you did to them, Emma?" Rose whispered once more as she slowly got to her feet.

"Uhm, well no I guess you probably don't want to know, hon."

"So Emma, getting back to Earth what are we going to do about the aliens there?" I asked now crawling out from my sleep chamber groggily, a slowly and carefully, still trying to get my legs to work after a year-long sleep.

"Well while you have been traveling here in your ship, sweeties, I have been back and forth to Earth to check things out. I have a plan that will see you down on the planet and safe for now and that will allow you to take your home from these aliens."

"So what's the plan?" I asked.

"Well, it's very simple really, dears. You see there are four alien ships around your planet. I will go and destroy them while you land in the safe place I have picked out for you. See? No problem at all."

Rose and I looked at each other with a nasty suspicion that all was not what it seemed. "Emma, what aren't you telling us?" Rose asked.

"Why whatever do you mean, dearest?"

"What Rose means, Emma, is that nothing that has

happened so far on this little adventure of ours has been easy or simple."

"No really, my dears, it is that simple. The place that you will land at is an island where I was born. The aliens seemed to have left that place alone and in fact, there seems to be a small band of Human survivors still there."

"How many people are there, Emma?" I asked.

"I'm sorry to say dears that there seem to be no more than one hundred of the Humans in this area, but it is near my old birthplace."

"Okay so can you show us where this place is?"

"Oh why of course sweeties how silly of me," Emma said as a map of a land mass showed up on the screen in front of us. *"This was what once was called the United States of America. And this point right here,"* a small dot popped up on the map, *"was called the Pacific Northwest."*

The screen moved in closer to the dot on the map and we could see that indeed it was sitting on the edge of a small island. "So what's so important about this little piece of land?" Rose asked as she leaned down and looked closer at the glowing dot.

"Well, dears, it seems that a long time ago this spot used to be an old naval air base and then was converted over to a test site for ships like me."

"There is no ship like you," Rose snickered under her

breath just loud enough for me to hear. I gave a small snort as I tried not to laugh out loud at my cousin's remark.

"Are you alright, dears?" Emma asked.

"Yeah, yeah, we're fine just dry throats from all that sleep, Emma," I answered.

"Oh well let me help, sweeties," she said as a panel opened up in the control console and two cans of liquid popped up like magic. *"And to let you know before you ask, the stuff in the cans are safe for you to drink. This ship seems to have been set up for human transportation before it was used in the planet's emergency."*

"That's fine, Emma, and thanks for the liquid, but back to this test area you were telling us about."

"Yeah, what Cassie said, Emma," Rose echoed back at the speaker above us in between sips from the can.

"Right, sorry sweeties. The base is on the island and is defended by self-sustained defenses so the aliens stay away from this island. I have found the passwords to let you get in and land and take over the base for your use. Once you are down and the ships in orbit are destroyed you can take out the aliens on the planet and take your world back."

"Uhm Emma you mean we can do that right? You are coming down with us to Earth?" Rose asked.

"Oh sure, hon, yes that is what I meant – when we get down to Earth. Now when you get down to Earth, I suggest that you first wake your parents from their sleep, before you wake everyone else up. They will tell you who in the group of Humans with you are the

leaders and will help you get set up."

"Why not go and wake everyone up at the same time?" I questioned.

"Well, you could do that, dear, except that then you will have to take care of five hundred people all at once coming out of sleep hibernation, where if you do it a bit at a time you will be sure to have someone there to help you."

"Yeah, okay, Emma, you win on that point, I guess. So when do we put this plan in action?" I asked.

"Well, dears it will take me about an hour to sneak up on those alien ships and get where I want to be so I want you to get something to eat and rest up for you are going to be very busy after that."

"Okay Emma," I said as I looked over at my cousin. "Come on Rose, dinner time." Then we both headed down to find some food to eat in this rust bucket we were trapped in.

An hour later we were fed, watered and buckled into the control chairs waiting for Emma to make her move on the alien ships. We were watching the four ships on the view screens as they now came together in one spot above the planet below us. I don't know if they had caught a whiff of Emma as she tried to sneak up on them or if she was luring them together to take them all out at once, but whatever it was I didn't like the looks of it.

"This is not good, Cassie; I think they know that she is out there."

"Yeah, I was thinking the same thing, Rose. How about we get out there and give them a little distraction so that Emma can take them out."

"Ready, dears?" Emma's voice suddenly sounded over the speaker above our head. Both Rose and I jumped in our seat as though we had been caught doing something wrong by our mother.

"Emma? What's going on, we're coming out there to help you," I said looking once more at the view screen in front of us.

"Yeah, well see sweeties that wouldn't be such a great idea, so I have locked you two out of the controls of the ship. . ."

"WHAT, YOU CAN'T DO THAT, EMMA!" I shouted at the speaker while Rose started to unbuckle herself from her chair. I don't know where she thought she was going, but I started to follow her lead when we were both jerked back into the seat from the acceleration and movement of the ship we were on.

"Yes well, dears, you have no choice in the matter now do you? The ship has been locked into taking you toward my birthplace even after I am gone, so I wanted to say that I love you both and will miss you."

"NO EMMA, DON"T DO THIS!" I heard Rose cry as we

passed by the alien ships and started to move around the planet below us. One of the alien ships started to change direction to intercept us when Emma popped up in the middle of their formation, sending a broadside of torpedoes and lasers into the ship. As we started to loop around the planet toward our landing spot, I saw the alien ship that was hit and halted in mid-stride, explosions and debris flying off into space.

"Remember sweeties, I love you both," I heard whispered over the speaker then the darkness of space was lit up by a brilliant light that encompassed all the ships. Then we were around the planet and coming down into the atmosphere.

I sat there dazed as I could hear the whimper of my cousin in the seat next to me. "Emma, Emma, answer me," I whispered to the speaker above us. With each call of her name, Rose whimpered louder then settled down into a steady stream of tears and sobs.

As the ship moved down through space and then the blue sky, I saw that we were indeed headed toward a small island. I looked around as much as I could and saw old ruins of buildings and what looked like a long tall bridge that crossed from the mainland to the island we were headed toward.

"Rose, Rose look at me." My cousin peeked up, her face tear stained and blotchy at my voice.

"She's dead, isn't she, Cassie?"

I glanced out the view screen and then back at my cousin. "Yeah, she is, Rose, but now I need your help. I can't have you falling apart on me, okay? Can you do that, can you keep it together and help me?"

"Yes I'll try, Cassie," she sniffed out then sat up straighter in her chair and squared her shoulders back. "Yes I will, I will help you. What do we do?"

"Well, first cousin we check out the surrounding area to make sure it's safe and then we do what Emma told us to do."

"Wake up your parents?"

"Yeah, wake up my parents."

Then we felt a gentle bump from touchdown and the rockets cut out. We sat there in silence looking out at the scenery around us. From our viewpoint, we could see that we had landed on a concrete pad or road and we could see a large storage building in front of us with the ocean behind it.

I sat there with Rose, both of us lost in our own thoughts when I heard a faint whisper —*well don't just sit there, hon, you have a job to do.* I looked over at Rose with some faint hope that she had heard the same whisper. "Did you hear that?"

"Hear what, Cassie?" Rose asked, looking at me with a puzzled stare.

"Nothing Rose, I guess I'm just tired. Come on we have a

job to do and we can't sit here all day long," I said as I stood.

"Okay, whatever you say, Cassie," Rose said as once more she got out of her chair and followed me down to the airlock of our ship.

We moved around the ship gathering what supplies and weapons we needed to make a quick reconnaissance around the transport before we woke anyone up from their long sleep. As the hatch opened in the quiet of the coming night, I could hear the strange sounds of birds and the buzzing of insects.

I slowly walked down the ramp while Rose kept an eye out from the hatch for any danger. Stepping down onto the ground, I looked up as my cousin followed me down and stood next to me. "Pretty isn't it, Cassie?"

"Yeah, and quiet too, Rose."

Rose looked around; her eyes wide with wonder as we watched the last of the bright daylight leave the sky. As night fell we stood there once more looking up into the darkness as a shower of sparks flew over our head in the star-filled night.

"Now what, Cassie?"

"Now we check around the area and then we go wake my parents. After that, we clean house of any aliens and take our home back, Rose," I said as I looked around the area before I headed toward the large building before me.

ABOUT THE AUTHOR

Robert Wright is the author of the "Witch Way" series, books written as young adult/fantasy. He is also busy writing a new sci-fi series starting with "Walk the Stars". His characters are based on drawings and doodles that he has worked on since he could pick up a pencil. Robert has traveled the world and met many interesting people but now lives in Bellingham, Washington with his wife and youngest child (along with his imaginary friend Percy, the dragon). Bellingham is the setting for "Witch Way Back" as well as the upcoming "Ruby Red and the Wolf" slated for release in early 2017. For more information on these enjoyable books please visit witchwaybooks.com or stop by the Witch Way Books page on Facebook.

Made in the USA
San Bernardino, CA
10 June 2016